Patterns

and other stories

EITHNE STRONG

poolbeg press

First published 1981 by
Poolbeg Press Ltd.,
Knocksedan House,
Swords, Co. Dublin, Ireland.

© Eithne Strong, 1981

Cover illustration by Cecil King
Design by Steven Hope

The generous assistance of An Chomhairle Ealaíon (The Arts
Council) and of the Arts Council of Northern Ireland in
the publication of this book is gratefully acknowledged.

Printed by Cahill Printers Ltd.,
East Wall Road, Dublin 3.

Contents

With acknowledgements to *The Irish Press* 'New Irish Writing', *Winter's Tales from Ireland*, *Best Irish Short Stories* and *Icarus* where some of these stories first appeared.

Patterns

When they came, Mrs. Teague asked if they were
hungry. Mechtildhe said, "On the plane we haf
eaten. We are not liking to eat . . . too much." Lisl
said, "We are not." They were tall and proudly lean.
As they walked they raised their ribs fastidiously,
elongating waists. Their absence of appetite may
have been a relief to Mrs. Teague. She exuded
shades of preoccupation. A plumping woman, with
her escaping air of private burden, she somehow
suggested the sort of person who might be given to
eating secret consolatory snacks while visited with
a cancelling adolescent brand of guilt. Her face
seemed to reflex continually in upward curves as
though trained in an effort against betrayal of inner
descendent tendencies.

One of her more bothering problems might have
been her daughter, Pamela, who, for five years,
came and went between her different men, using
her parents' house as a scattering area. This time,
she had come three days ago with her baby. The

child's father, she said, was playing reasonably fair; they had agreed to split up; he was providing some money; she did not wish to be at all obliged to him; they were tolerable friends. She had, she went on to tell her parents, arranged to link shortly with her latest man who, having left Hampstead, had bought a place in a Kerry bog, and there they were to live basic, natural lives: they were both sick of pollution and commercialism. She had then proceeded, as usual, to spill an assortment of soft baggage at unpredictable points about the house. As usual, it appeared impossible to curb the flow and several curious cloth bags and gingham bundles —her chosen portmanteaux—still lay around the hall. The German travelling-cases, blooming a factory burnish of yellow plastic, stood neatly new by the foot of the stairs.

"This," said Mrs. Teague, "is Pamela. The one you have never met."

This year, the German cousins were a new pair. They made, each, a little scented nod to Pamela. "Hi," she said very amusedly, giving them her sideways smile through a swathe of red hair. With vivid fingers she twitched away from bare feet, none too clean, a frayed edge of skirt. It could seem that her manner was less than casual.

"Michael," Mrs. Teague said, speaking of her husband, "is busy out there." She flickered an indefinite hand towards the rear of the house. "Later, you will see him."

"Yess," Mechtildhe said. Lisl said, "So!"

The attenuating blood-bond between ramifying branches of Teagues and Müllers had latterly tended to become reduced to the dimensions of expediency. Everyone was, by this stage, a little confused about respective identities; all manner of changes seemed to have been accelerating so madly. Dispensing with unnecessary affirmations of cousinship, Teagues and Müllers continued to use as holiday venues, with a cool but proper understanding, one another's households. For example, a Teague, one with leanings to thermodynamics, had that morning flown out to a Müller base near Dusseldorf. In the time of the grandparents, correct letters, carrying, notwithstanding, some real affection, were exchanged a few times a year; nowadays, affection, unless freshly stimulated, had thinned, though the periphery of formality was judiciously observed. Pamela, after a teenage visit to the Munich Müllers—which she herself cut short before a week was out: she had always shown aberrant traits—had never since given the slightest hint of a wish to resume those particular cousinly contacts.

Mrs. Teague, the corners of her top lip and wings of her nose going upwards to refuse a small frown threatening between her eyebrows, said, "How are you all now since . . ." She stopped not so much unhappily as uncomfortably.

"Since our mother iss dead?" Mechtildhe said.

"Yes . . . I really must come over soon . . ."
Mrs. Teague's voice dried in an onset of barrenness. She was looking at a point beyond the two girls where Pamela had dropped cross-legged on the floor to suckle her child. The small girl looked about twelve months old. She was totally naked.

"Since our mother iss dead," Mechtildhe said carefully, "we are doing everythink very well."

"Yess," said Lisl. "My older sister," she added in the direction of Pamela, "gif her baby a cup for trink."

Pamela played a flap of her marvellous red hair over the child's brown body. "I give my baby a bone," she said and laughed.

"What you say bone?"

"I will not say it more than once," Pamela continued to be amused, "but I'll tell you what I *will* do. I'll show you where Mother is putting you." She got to her feet in a liquid movement, the child sucking undisturbed. The German cousins regarded each other with something less than composure. Pamela invited them through a passage where a large checked blanket was knotted into a sort of nest from which spilled a miscellany of garments. The two girls delayed a tentative moment by their cases before picking them up and following. "You may as well, indeed," said Mrs. Teague. She remained standing absolutely still, briefly, and then she said, "You are quite immune." To whom was unclear as the others were already out of hearing.

The room to which Pamela led the cousins was up a flight of steps and looked out over a tangled garden.

"You can keep your eye on Father here," she told them, pointing outside. A wood and glass hut, covered in vinery, was distinguishable from the window. Along the side of the hut, a puppy-dog kept leaping over and over at a tantalising flutter of withered creeper. He was barking crazily and a greyish stir, occurring behind the glass, connected with a voice requesting remotely, "Quiet, little chap, quiet." The pup continued as before until a swooping seagull distracted him.

"Michael," said Mrs. Teague, who had now followed into the room, "is writing a book . . ."

". . . about placing the counter-culture," butted in Pamela. "I am his living source. Isn't that right, Mother?"

Her mother went to the window, looked down

at the uncertain grey stir, then back at Pamela who was now wearing the child, asleep, in a brilliant green cotton sling. She said nothing.

Twenty minutes after their arrival, Mechtildhe and Lisl, slenderly formidable, were prepared. Already, their travelling clothes hung creaselessly in the shared wardrobe; their yellow cases were unpacked and, extraordinarily, out of sight: the small room was regimented into two strict areas, one to each girl; their nine or ten pairs of shoes apiece were ranged in two rigid rows of remorseless femininity, trees of the most recent design stretching taut the variously processed surfaces. The holiday was unequivocally begun, in impeccable sequence. Zipped within jeans predatorily intent over mons and buttock, they flashed whitely down the stairs and into the summer afternoon.

"That was very speedy of you," Mrs. Teague remarked from a border, her hands inept with a bunch of ravelled garden twine. A quality of arranged appreciation came with the remark. "You are off somewhere?" The question, a mere gambit, a trifle tired, thinned away, wishing no answer. But an energetic reply was immediate from Mechtildhe. "There iss someone I must find." She looked compellingly at Lisl. "Our other sister gif him our mother's ring last time. This she should not haf done. Our mother meant this ring for me when she iss dead." "Really?" Mrs. Teague appeared to give little weight to the matter. "What a good thing the afternoon is fine," she irrelevantly commented. "So," Lisl decided.

Sitting at an upstairs window, Pamela was singing "All For The Sake Of My Little Nut-Tree" to the mauve sky.

The German pair took the harbour road. Mrs.

Teague looked after their deliciously swaying fragile waists. A clump of mothers, hung with seaside impedimenta and fractious young at the bus-stop, stared after their icy grace. A low orange sports-car tooted them and, having passed, pulled into the pavement ahead.

When they returned it was in the orange car.

"That," Mechtildhe informed Mrs. Teague to the tune of its retreating triumph, "iss our new friend. Not Irish. American. Tomorrow, he will take us to see. He hass this car. It is agreeable to see with car."

"So," Lisl agreed. No further mention was made of any ring. They ran to their room and very soon reappeared in a total change of attire; waves of fugitive fragrance drifted about them.

Pamela lifted her crawling child out of a sugar-bowl and poised her near the table-edge.

"You haf not her yet in bed?" Mechtildhe censured, drawing herself to safer distance; the child was making sugary grabs at the air. "She will fall," Lisl said with clear relish. Pamela, regardless, watched the pup eating through a stuffed toy which he relinquished in favour of Lisl's bright feet. Out of no concern for the pretty footwear but rather out of the moment's caprice, it appeared, Pamela stooped and picked up the frisking animal, petting him. "In Shermany, all shiltren are goink to bed . . . most early," Mechtildhe declared, regarding the child in plain distaste. "Men diforce vifes who are not putting shiltren to bed."

"Was that," Pamela was pert, "why your mother got divorced?"

Mechtildhe, unoffended, grew heavily serious. "No," she said, "becoss my father was what you say horreeble. We do not know him now. He iss killingk my mother."

Pamela dropped her head, a screen of her hair falling over the small dog. He began to eat it at one shoulder. "Dogs," Lisl said, "haf sherms." Pamela allowed the pup the other shoulder while the baby offered Lisl a jab of dribbled butter. Mrs. Teague, coming in, said with mustered cheer, "You must indeed be hungry." She held out a bowl of fruit. "Michael is bringing . . . something."

Michael Teague, grey, protected behind abstracted glasses, advanced. He bowed to the cousins. In one hand he was carrying a blue porcelain jar with a bamboo handle. "Have a cockle, my dear," he suggested to the room generally, and then focussing vaguely on the German girls, rattled the jar in their neighbourhood. He seemed either accustomed or indifferent to encountering feeble response. When the two made no move to his proferring jar beyond a negative glazed "thank you," he proceeded, enshrouded in a sort of cloud of unknowing, to the table where he rattled at the baby. "Give her a couple to bang around, you could," Pamela suggested.

"You *know* I hate the things, Michael." Mrs. Teague looked pained before the advancing jar. "Well, you do, of course," her husband admitted, "but nevertheless . . . you could change." He coughed a papery laugh.

"I will make you all some jasmine tea in a minute," Pamela unexpectedly said, "when I'm finished with this." She had lugged the large checked blanket inside the room and was rapidly squashing its contents into a long tubular hessian bag, like a monstrous pale brown slug. Her cousins, seeing the operation, appeared to be at a loss for any apt expression. Mrs. Teague was attempting rudimentary things with the cluttered table. "Now," Pamela said, clinching a tough rope knot—she sounded well satisfied—"that's ready. Notice, Father. I actually *can* be ready if I choose. It *is* worth noticing that we do have our own sort of pattern."

"Yes." Her father's eyes stayed on her, momentarily. "But the pattern, for all its boasted freedom from tyranny—your frequent boast—is almost always an imposition on other people. You express your pattern, in this house, at our expense—of occasion, location, convenience . . ." His tone was mild. He shook the cockle-jar speculatively, eyebrows lifted in an inward look.

Pamela handed round the light tea. When she came to her father, she gently took the jar from him and set it, attentively, out of danger's reach. "You, Father," she said, "who are always emphasising that life is change, consider how good I am for you. To have firsthand knowledge of such change as I afford you, in what could be—no offence—a fossilising existence, is fulfilling for you."

He tasted the tea, making no answer, eyes shielded behind glasses. Mrs. Teague broke into a fervent burst. "Pamela, you *must* dress this child."

"I like her naked. Her responses will be much freer."

"You *will* dress her for the train?"

Pamela thought for a moment. "Yes . . . because the evening will get chillier."

"You are goink?" Mechtildhe queried.

"Goingk?" echoed Lisl.

"Yes, I am going to my new house in the country."

Mechtildhe appeared to ponder; then, she said, "We would wish to see such a house before we are returning to Shermany . . . real Irish country."

"You can come so long as you are ready to be . . ." Pamela gave the two cousins a lightning mocking look, "like me—which, of course, you are; sleep

anywhere; liberate from the compulsion of stero-
type, from stodgy possessions;immerse in the mud;
fraternise with cows. It is a cowhouse. The cows
are still in it. We are going to change, build, extend
it ourselves," she ended climactically.

"You haf water?"

"There is a well. Splendid possibilities."

"You haf light?"

"Candles, oil-lamps. We will make a wind-
charger. The place," Pamela enlarged happily, deck-
ing her child in a minute garment embroidered in
Indian mirror-work, "is in the middle of nowhere."

"You haf car?"

"So far, a donkey and cart. Ha-ha-ha."

"So!" Lisl contributed. Mechtildhe seemed
stimulated. "Next year," she expanded, *we* haf a
new house. We join with some of our cousins
to buy it. All flats;luxury, everythink new. Electric.
I design all inside. My job you see. Thees American
today haf big interest in Sherman design. Much
money. Much comfort." She circled a beautiful
foot in its delicate shoe, without any doubt well-
pleased with her appendages.

Pamela jumped up in a vigorous swing of hair
and petticoats—she seemed to be carrying about
four liquefying layers of skirt—yet in an indefinable
way her movement seemed to reject visible trammels
of hair and skirt. It was as if she were disengaging
herself from palpable effects. A conspicuous hole
showed in the front of one layer of skirt. She held
up the cloth, deliberately displaying the hole. Then,
with a downward whisk of her hand, she brushed
the material into the line of her limbs, dismissing
the external flaw as non-existent, or of no account.

"Why, oh, why, Pamela," her mother's voice was
the sound of one in pain, "must you go about like

a tinker? I really have kept patience, to bursting. But, really—you are the absolute end. You have, or could have, just loads of perfectly decent things."

"Mother, am I harming anyone? You? Anyone? Perhaps I *am* a bit disturbing to calcified mores but . . . haven't I my own tattered charm?"

She curved extravagantly, teasingly, under her mother's face. The child, again in her sling at Pamela's side and therefore moulded to her movements, chortled at the caper.

"Your whole style," Mrs. Teague was saying, the reflexes in her face-muscles seeming a little weary of their upward conditioning, "is an affectation—as aggravating as any; as anything you can name in the gin and vodka belt you profess to mock at."

"Mother darling, you and Father will take me to the station in good grace, now, even so?" Pamela sang, in apparent airy unconcern, rushing to gather the pup to her free side.

"Don't we help you in every way, whenever at all possible? You know perfectly well we'll be taking you to the train. Michael?"

Michael Teague was meticulously polishing his glasses. "I am," he said, breaking the sentence to arrange the glasses over careful eyes, "ready."

"You might like to come for the ride," Mrs. Teague said to the cousins. They both said a simultaneous "Yess."

The station-wagon, moving away from the door, looked laden.

At the station, a vast crush of football fans was returning south. The guard refused to take the pup in his van on the grounds that he was "not properly confined". Pamela, a complex of hair, baby, and layered skirts, was somehow stowed inside a massed

14

carriage. Her bare feet were excessively vulnerable. A couple of maudlin hands made an unsure show of steadying her and a voice going with them said, "Yerra in shure, 'tis a bit airly for Killorglin." A Kerryman with searing breath, to whom also belonged the hands and voice, exhorted his companions, "Now bhyes, can't ye push over in the doss an' make room for the people." He extended his ministrations to pulling in the long, stuffed slug of Pamela's belongings, and to clutching the panting pup to his chest. "I'll mine him now for oo girrl," he comforted Pamela, "I'll mine him," he insisted, redly benign.

The German cousins feathered elegantly restrained kisses towards Pamela as the train chugged out.

On the way back, Michael Teague drove slowly, straining into the darkening road. Mrs. Teague was entirely quiet.

"Next year," Mechtildhe said, a thought doubtfully, "Pamela can haf change with us in our beautiful electric clean place."

Thursday To Wednesday

Like a fever in the blood, this wanting to go further. What were the territories behind the frontiers of eyes and conversational gambit? The routine demands of noses to be wiped, shoelaces tied, chores organised, squabbles broken up, were not enough to hold her steady. Like a thirst. Like an appetite hungry since yesterday. New ground for questing.

Nora came into the room and threw herself on to her mother's bed, her dark eyes watchful, aware. She knew.

"It's all a big plot, isn't it Mummy?"

"What is, my darling?"

No answer. Her face showed its knowing. The mother turned her disconcertion to the mirror and saw there her daughter still watchful. Oh for an unbetraying pale skin: flushing conveys unsureness, guilt. She should not have to feel guilty. What wrong was there in wanting to go out with him? Spend a few hours in his company? "It is ridiculous that I shouldn't feel free to do so," she was telling herself. "Why is she so jealous and watchful of me still and all the latitude she has been allowed to work out her own things?" She resented the unspoken censure from her daughter and also, immediately, was self-critical because of this resentment.

Rubbing make-up on to her face, she observed Nora in the mirror, while trying to find inside herself a balance, trying to surmount the troubling urgency; wondering was this, after all, another instance like so many other countless instances where she must submerge herself for the good of the general. Would she be harming Nora, her half-formed standards of values? Was she not accountable for many troubles and puzzlements in the girl's so-far journey into adolescence? True maybe. True very likely. But her own journey into ever expanding life was often over uncharted areas. She was often confused and troubled herself but always convinced that she should go on.

As she stood there before the mirror her stomach went heavy in sudden sickness. She went on fixing up her eyes, thinking, as she drew a pencil around their careful blankness, that she was a silly woman. She was really like anyone else who went in for hole-and-corner only she was giving what she did a pretentious build-up: the ultimate good of human inter-relationship; advancement through understanding in the man-woman field and such-like. It was presumptuous to assume she was progressing beyond Mrs Suburban-married who steadily kept to the humdrum limits of social acceptability. Yes, I am a self-engrosed woman, giving myself airs.

"Where are you going Mummy?" Katherine came to jog on the edge of the bed.

"But you, *all* of you, knew I was going out tonight. I had asked Nora, two days ago, to be free for baby-sitting."

"But where?" Katherine insisted.

Nora said: "You are not going to the play—I know there were no bookings left. Then well . . . ?"

"I'm still going out," she heard the strain in her voice. In spite of the bothering thoughts and heavy stomach, she had decided to go.

"But where?" Katherine was not letting up.

"I'm not quite sure really. Just out. Out for the evening."

Nora got off the bed and went downstairs. Through the curtains her mother could see her sitting beside him on the garden seat. She was lengthened out seductively, a show of creamy flesh between short skinny rib sweater and jeans. He was noticing her. The mother thought: there she is, acting my rival—in spite of her thing with Greg, she is deliberately displaying her potential to a man who, she knows, likes me. It has all happened before. The old pattern. Any man interested in me will be made particularly aware of her lusciousness.

Nora's face was secret, unhappy, as she gave him a speculative sideways glance.

The mother, finally ready, went downstairs. The two small ones ran from the kitchen.

"Mummy, Mummy. I don't want you to go out."

"Nora will put you to bed tonight."

"No no. I want you to put us to bed. I want you to read us the story."

"Katherine will read the story."

"No no no. *You* must read the story."

"If you come straight to bed then, this minute, I'll read you a story."

"I don't want to go to bed now."

"But sweethearts, you can't have it every way. I'll put you to bed now and read you a story or else I go out immediately and Nora will put you to bed later—with a story then."

"Where are you going?"

"Oh—just—out. Out for the beginning, later there is a party I have been asked to."

She hugged and kissed them. They made small attempts at crying, wanting to keep her longer, but she went out into the garden.

He got up from the seat and followed her to the car. Nora came to the gate looking slantways from her mother, a small cynical smile shaping her mouth. The mother was very unhappy. She wished that as she was there in the car ready to go, with him beside her, they would all wave and smile at her, as they always did when everything was in tune. Nora shouldered the gate-post and, when her mother, with mustered courage, looked full at her, met the look with a glassiness. She was her mother's child. She was also someone who, the mother felt, was at that moment seeing her through the remembered perspective of difficulties she had hoped were resolved between them.

He was looking at Nora; the girl's eyes moved to him. Was that a flicker of conspiracy in her look? In the lightning instant it took to think such a thing, the mother wondered was there something between them. Were they leagued in mockery against her? She let her hair fall over to hide whatever the horrible feeling in her chest was doing to her face and turned away to twist down the car-window. Katherine stood by it.

"Where are you going Mummy?"

"I'm not sure darling—out—just—' She did not want to keep on trying to give a truthful answer;

19

she was afraid to use her voice any more. She bent her head sideways through the window for the usual goodbye kiss from Katherine. The car moved off and she noticed how he looked back at Nora.

Suddenly she felt like stopping, getting out, letting him move from now entirely on his own impetus. The outing was partly her engineering but she had gone to the trouble of fixing it because of some indications that he would like it.

In silence she drove for several minutes, aware that he was studying her. The earlier urgency to be alone with him had sunk right down beneath a weight of confusion.

Old troubled stuff between Nora and me. I had hoped all that fester lanced, cleanly healed. Wrong of me to start off her memory of the wound. Hostility of daughter towards mother is only abeyant, not resolved . . . this driving-out with him can stir it, cause it to threaten what I had hoped was surer understanding. A stupid business, this making off with him, especially if what I fancied just now . . . that look he gave her, she gave him . . . or maybe I'm suspicious because I'm jealous of my own blossoming daughter. Natural enough that he might feel drawn to both of us . . . we complement one another, different qualities. If things could only be more openly said and done. Anyway Nora is so greatly preoccupied with Greg, this present thing probably touches her only as another lightly taken for granted acclaim to her power of youth.

The mother, nevertheless, felt at this moment a dismal feebleness against such power. She was very still in her body while her mind churned over. Automatically she watched the road and shifted gears.

"Hello," he suddenly leaned forwards and to-

20

wards her, the better to see her face. "How are you?"

Earlier in the day, or on any of the previous days since they had met, she would have answered such inquiry lightly, flippantly. Now she said:

"At the moment a bit involved . . ."

"So."

He had known it anyway. He sat back and did not speak any more until they passed someone he recognised from Brompton. With the easy light surprise of the well-travelled, much removed from the exclamatory astonishment of the insular Irishman, he said,

"It's that face from The Three Bells. Many a day I have watched him eating veal and ham pie." As if it were the most natural transition for that face now to be parading along Sandycove. She asked,

"Do you want to say hello? I'll pull in if you wish."

"No no. Not at this moment." He put a hand on her knee. In the lounge overlooking Coliemore Harbour, while they each sipped something, he said, "Your nervousness at leaving home was very apparent."

"Nervousness is too simple a description. It was much more than that."

"Tension then?"

"Yes, tension, and yet more." She looked across the harbour where one solitary motor-boat and its attendant skier ripped through the calm surface. A picture of Nora's face came before her mind's eye and this time, surprisingly, there came with it the first ease that evening. The heaviness lightened in her stomach. She looked back at him. "You see I put the children before everything else, that is after Brian. I hate hugger-mugger if you know—well, I hate deceiving. I couldn't explain to the children about you and this evening—having a drink out and that—Brian, of course, knows anyway. But the children, with them it's more complicated. There have been issues before, decisions to be made about—many things. I have found in trying to work them out as honestly as I know, that, well, that I have had to face up to much bother about personal wholeness—integrity is the usual word, I suppose. There has been much pain involved you know, and a—well—anything that comes near to stirring that sort of hurt into remembrance—it's not so easy you see. So therefore, nervousness is not exactly the word. You saw the outer side of—maybe covered trouble, if you like."

He was listening and looking, it seemed, with all attention, and then he turned towards the water-skier. That made her wonder had she been boring him. What *was* really behind the frontiers of eyes? But he looked away again from the skier and back to her, saying,

"Yes I hear. I think I have understood."

She felt perhaps he had. She also felt that, if need be, she could say out to him about her feeling involving Nora, himself and herself.

Afterwards, going to the car, he said, "I love your family you know."

"It always surprises me, but people seem to, in spite of the rows . . . not *all* people of course. We are too chaotic."

"I have seen no rows."

"You haven't been with us long enough. The rows are bloody. I never believe in families that are just *so nice* all the time—some fur and feather flying is healthier; anyway I have to say that to console myself for lack of control . . ." They were

in the front seat and she stopped abruptly because
he was not listening, only watching her. She was
not proof against this; a kiss after that kind of looking was as natural as one breath after another.
Gently she pulled at his tie.

"I know it's for the party later but I would
prefer . . ." she began to undo the knot. He ripped
the tie from his neck. She opened the buttons at
the top of his shirt. He began also, impatiently, to
undo them himself but she said, "Please let me. I
want to." His chest was dark-skinned and thickly
hairy. "A jungle," she put her face down to the
dark hairiness. The last button about the trouser-
belt. "All the way," she said.

"No no. I would be cold." He joked all the time
covering up feeling. "You are very passionate," he
was keeping her hands.

"I hardly think more than you."

"No no. I am not passionate." Another joke.
Who had searched in the kissing? A small doubt
moved in her.

"So you are not passionate? All right. Suits me
fine." She would play his game a little.

"Women frighten me."

"Poor little thing." She remembered he had also
said it the first day they had spoken together: a
rather laboured sort of fun. "So they frighten poor
little boy." She would continue in this way for a
while. It could become less laboured. "And why do
they?"

"Because I am impotent."

"Oh poor boy. Well neither can I make love."

Silence.

He bent his head low, nuzzling over the summer
dress. The windows of the car were fogged over but
some light shone from the harbour wall. Cars flashed

all the time as people drove in and out of the parking space.

"We'll move out of here," she said. They drove to a place over the city, silence continuing between them. She watched the lights all around the bay. In her quietness an unhappiness was vaguely settling back on her. They did not touch. She said, "What do you want with me?" She was already detaching herself from an expectation of the promise she felt might have been contained in him. Why should she have needed anything really, who had had so much? And what of that earlier pounding fever?

Very quickly there blurred through her mind thoughts about the degrees in which they had circled nearer to one another over the few days since they had met. Her first reaction to him had been that his face told of great suffering. Yet when he spoke it was nearly always in drollery. She had felt a certain pity but nothing animal had stirred in her towards him. Later in the day, he went with their large family party on a picnic. She had come suddenly upon him lying in swarthy hairiness, sunning himself. The unexpectedness of so much hair repelled her. As she knelt on the grass and he moved easily, good-humouredly submitting to the tugs of children, she knew a query in herself: could she ever be drawn to caress this body? At that time she felt that she could not.

Through the first evening he ragged all the time. Most things he said had some bearing on her; motherhood, fertility, good management. Mocking but harmless; no barbs. Any time she looked towards him, his eyes were already on her. She remained reserved, trying to add him up.

Later that night a party of them were to meet in a Dublin pub. When she got there he had already had a few. He started on the compliments game but she was determined to get him off trivialities. She managed; his coherence on more consequential matters, his way of thinking, pleased her. His odd fatuous remark on her shape or looks did not bother her; they were part of the tune most men in the place had for the women with them, by this time of the evening. The other things he had to say made her feel there was much to him she wanted to know about.

As they tried to stand their ground on the crowded floor, his hand, steadying, gripped hers. She felt herself answering with tightened fingers. On the way home in a packed car she found herself squashed on to his lap. He kissed her hair and neck and even though she made no response, she liked it.

She was staking gladioli next day when he appeared; he fiddled about and did a few small helpful things. She was quiet, wondering about the night before and his extra drinks. And he spoke hearing her thoughts, maybe.

"It's a pity, not much talk today. No booze?"

"So that's what you think?"

"Well it's the essential oil, isn't it?"

"Not for me."

"Good. Actually I don't like pubs; my friends go there and so—sometimes I go."

The whole of the day some quality was in the air between them. All the time they were with other people, but it was there. A sliding look, a hand brushing in the traffic of meals, silences, part-said things, and always the drollery which sometimes baffled her. Once in a doorway he held a match to her cigarette and at such close quarters, she found all of herself answering him. All of her stirred then.

In a carful they went down the country. She held

a lolling child in her lap; beside her he sat, controlled and removed in his corner of the seat. Once or twice in the longish trip she felt his fingers on her arm. He could as easily have taken her hand. She wondered why he hadn't. Nervous of being seen by Brian in the driving-mirror? He would not know, of course, that already she had told Brian she was drawn to him, was curious about him. People are so conditioned to the idea of deceiving husbands and wives. Why deceive? Because openness might suggest commitment? It is easier to have surreptitious indulgences. Pleasure living. She was already judging him to be in the category of pleasure takers and she knew nothing of him. Why the devil, she started to ask herself, should *I* judge? Even I, in my imagined emancipation, find myself still tuned to self-righteousness.

The sleeping child stirred restlessly in her lap. She wrapped him closer in her arms thinking: one absolute thing this, anyhow, over which there need be no doubt, no scrutiny—the caring for child by mother. And even with this clear thought she knew simultaneously a retrograde wish to be, at that moment, free of the child and his undoubted need of her, so that she might herself turn in enticement to the man beside her.

When they got home he said he was going into the town. Natural; his other friends from the London group were there. "If you, of course," he said, backing, "care to join us later—that would, needless to say, be our great pleasure."

What verbal flourish when he so chooses! Immediately she decided against going. She felt depressed now. How unaccountable the compound of a make-up, she self-assessed in some contempt for her own fluctuations. There was much to be done; she had three callers in the house that evening needing her attention. There were a hundred and one things to be seen to over a meal and general family doings. She put depression away behind a determined activity. Later when the house was quiet and Brian had gone to write some letters, she played a gloomy Scandinavian record. Nora came in.

"Why are you playing that awful ghostly music?"

Why indeed.

It was getting late, on for midnight. He will have gone to some party; will, very likely, be out until all hours. She had just finished making a list for the next day's supplies when he came back. Nora had said goodnight twice by this time and gone upstairs; she now returned downstairs and stayed around for one small contrived reason or another. Her mother felt she was keeping guard and although she understood the necessity in the girl, it irked her, this watchfulness. Some hardness in her resolved to outstay Nora; determined to see for once something she willed occur. So often the things she willed were thwarted, sometimes because she saw that what she initially willed, if carried out, would not be for the general best; sometimes through sheer crassness of circumstance. Just now her will was hard and clear, she would not this night yield to the censure which emanated from Nora. Her child was judging her from a remembered battleground which, at times, still seemed to space between them.

The mother went out to the garden where, in the light from the house, she began to collect littered odd toys. He followed her, helping.

"I'm going up now Mum, goodnight."

Nora's call through the open door was in her most usual voice, easy, non-measuring.

"Goodnight Nora." The third goodnight they had said to one another. Did I sound a nuance too casual with this one?

When they returned inside the house he stood there, waiting, while she put toys away and bolted the door for the night. Then they closed towards one another briefly, silently. After, she went to bed where Brian was already alseep.

All the next day she was busy; children, food, people, organising this and that, becoming vague, absent-minded in the pile-up of event. But at the back of it all was this distant fever beating in some recess of her. Time was short. Soon he would be gone. She could have just the one evening with him.

"Would you like it?" she had asked him.

"Of course, of course."

"We could link up with the others later . . ." she put tentatively, not wanting to seem as if taking possession of the evening.

"We'll see—perhaps—but—we'll see."

And that was how it had been. So here they now were, looking down at the city while she asked him, "What do you want with me?"

And he was answering, "I like you. I like to be with you."

She was afraid to ask the question she really wanted to put, so she went around it.

"When you are close to somebody what do you want?"

He considered.

"I am like you maybe, this feline quality—you like to stroke. I too, I like to touch. This nearness is necessary."

But he did not stroke nor touch any more.

"Women frighten me."

It was the third time he had said it.

She started the car and began to drive down towards the city.

"We'll go and find the others," she said, "this party should be beginning by now."

"Please, not the party. I don't want it. I'd rather stay with you. But you—perhaps you want to go?"

"No, I don't especially want to."

"Then please—with you."

She turned into a deserted hedged lane and switched off the engine.

"Shall we go in the back?" she asked, surprising herself.

"The back is very nice," was all he had to say. She had always hated "very nice".

"I love your enthusiasm," she said and he met that with a sudden return of drollery, shouting in pseudo-élan,

"Fo' Chrissake, the back is *lovely*!"

"Shh." Mostly something jarred in her when people called on Christ that way. He will find me impossible to please.

"You see," he said, "I don't like cars. Cars are awful. I hate cars."

"So a car is what we have."

"Yes and it is no good."

When his flesh was bared she bent to kiss. And again the question rose in her. This time she asked it.

"You *were* joking, weren't you?"

"Actually I have not had much success this way."

She kissed again the soft limp place, knowing great pity. Poor fellow. All that joking.

"I told you women frighten me."

"Yes, now I believe you. But all the time you fooled so much about everything—"

"I am so sorry to disappoint you."

"Shh, please do not be. I really only wish to know you. This—does not—matter."

"I am always guilty, fearful."

"I surely cannot be frightening to you?"

"I know, but it is always this way."

"Maybe if you thought more about the other person—" she ventured, "if you could *give* yourself—"

He was silent and then said, "It's right of course, what you say. I know it but I cannot do it." And after a minute he went on, "Also, a car is awful. One must have time and space. I hate a car."

"I agree entirely. Don't worry. It is cold; cover yourself."

They drove back to the city, searching without much interest for the place where the party was to be. Many times he put a hand on her knee, an excusing, pleading hand.

"It's all right," she said, "I like you very much even so."

"Please, please, not *even so*."

"Indeed it was not a good way to say it. I *like* you. Don't worry."

"Tonight, I'll stay in town—my plane is so early tomorrow."

"I know. You might as well book in somewhere soon. I can't find this party place."

"The party, the party, I never wanted to go to it."

They stopped near the bridge.

"I have a feeling," she said, "we were so near to something and we missed. I don't mean just—bodies."

"It was the car," he said and laughed a short unhappy laugh. His last joke. "No, not true. Not all true anyway. And I did—believe me—come closer

30

to you than to most."

He touched her mouth, "Goodbye then," and he was out on the pavement, walking away. He looked sad in the empty street. She drove the other way.

The Bride Of Christ

About three weeks gone now, the term. The students did not all have their uniforms yet. It took the tailor close on six weeks from the first measurement to get them all covered. Not that the measuring made very much difference to the final turn-out. Square long-sleeved garment to the waist. Navy serge. "Blouse" it was called in the college prospectus. A shapeless overdress of the same material hung to the calves. In over twenty years the outline had not changed.

"Ugly" assessed Sister Benignus in the silence of her cold detachment. "But what does it matter what they wear? Marking time."

She walked along by the wall where the September figs were ripening. Away on the far side beyond the trellised clematis they were at recreation. Games were compulsory. Sauntering groups were forbidden during recreation. The girls from Dingle were good at camogie; their rapid Irish urgent with the game came to her, their fluency of throaty aspiration, liquid diphthong and beautiful attenuation giving the tongue its living grace. Listening to them, richly vocal in the spontaneity of the playing-field, was one of the few things left that she liked. They could not see her through the screening clematis.

Outside of the class proper, English was allowed for only one half-hour in the day, the last one before evening silence and prayers. Accents from all over the country. But English as spoken by the Dingle girls was like a third language. What they wrote in it would be mostly correct, if stilted; this she knew for she had been given their papers to mark. But when they spoke it they made their own of it, in cadence and lilt and phraseology. It would have been scarcely intelligble to her own urbanised family, she sometimes thought.

Only now and then did she stop and face squarely towards the field; mostly she allowed the mixed noises from it to filter through her thinking while she walked, hands folded into deep sleeves, face well back in the recess of her veil.

"Clodhoppers, culchies," most surely that would have been Julia's opinion of them. In her mind she could hear that particular daughter's voice, the most incisive in the family, "God, what a life! How can girls *live* this way? It can't be called *living*. They don't know a thing . . . two, three years in this dump, wearing clothes like that—I wouldn't be seen dead in such a freakish get-up."

"Well, they *are* fulfilling a function," Sister Benignus parried, in the safety of the mental juxtaposition, with its emotional detachment from Julia, and purely for the sake of argument since her convictions concerning the matter were null. "They are *good* girls. They will teach the rising young."

"Good?" Julia was contemptuous. "Do you

mean good holy or good working?"

"It's a point," answered her mother with an open-mindedness that this mental argument favoured. "Considering it, I would say most likely both; most of them anyway. That is, when 'holy' means observing the rituals of making the sign of the cross before class, before meals; gabbling some automatic noises called prayers; never, never missing Mass; never giving scandal by a, possibly quite sincere, love experiment; sticking to the required observances. Yes, this bunch of girls will probably answer all the holy requirements. *And* are likely to work more or less as is demanded of them; often desperate enough, trying to cover the quota for the Department inspectors. Imagination? Even if they have it they will scarcely have the courage to substantiate it. Imagination is dangerous to religiously established tenets and to be checked at first evidence."

"But what life is it?"

"Depends how you see it. Contempt is arbitrary, and any life can be despised if we want to despise it. Is your sophistication more of an answer?"

"For me at present, no doubt about it; yes. You can have this lot any time."

"In fact, I think," Sister Benignus went on discursively, "there are some among them a bit like yourself but without your heritage of freer thought; these won't answer to the acceptable standard, in all likelihood, but will shape a bit after their own fancy. Sooner or later they bump into the trouble of their own punishing guilt and the censure of the powers that be. Probably the greater bulk of them, the abiders, the holy ones if you like, will make the strongest teachers in the long run. The most consistent. And isn't that what's needed in the country?" Sarcasm, cover for feeling, was gaining ground. She did not want to be disturbed to feeling. She wished no further involvement than the non-involvement of letting time pass. Anyway (in this mental projection of dialogue) Julia did not seem interested sufficiently to answer. Nevertheless her mother persisted in the same strain:

"The wayward Irish need a narrow consistency. Otherwise the growing young might find themselves imbalanced in a horrible jeopardy of experimental living and thinking. Iron strictures are the necessity of mad imaginations. That is a Church axiom. A people of tyranny and cowardice! And of them I am one. Therefore I can mock, criticise, condemn, propound, theorise, to my satisfaction. Not that it avails me or them in any way."

But Julia had left.

A bell signifying the end of recreation sounded from the convent. Not always lady-like the sounds that issued from those teachers-in-the-making at the end of play.

"Raucous," Sister Benignus thought, "and something else. What? What else is it that they are? Animals? Yes. Dogs. Only human dogs. Snarling animals. Teachers in the making. They are putting away the balls, the camogie sticks, the racquets and croquet mallets, these last symbols of a refinement removed from animals. Personified in Mother Evangeline. Belonging to another generation, she is nonplussed by this rough-raw material. The day of the West Briton is definitely finished. She presides only because of the prestige of her seniority. Soon she will be replaced. The Dingle girls will not make croquet-players. Never. Maybe some of the aspiring socialites from other parts will?

"The wallop of a camogie-stick; cows massing through a gap in the ditch. My children were like this. Walloping, crowding. Only I relinquished command. Trying for a gentler control in reaction against regimentation, I lost direction; bogged down. Swamped. I was beaten. Their fierce uncontrol triumphed. I have accepted failure. In the end they all went their own ways. I was needed no more. They were gone. Then Alec dead. Often I wished to be dead. Why he first? Was it fair? He left me without any final resolution between us. We never worked the thing out. I think the facade appeared whole. I think so. No one knew. Only the two of us knew the defeat, the problem unsolved. The unbridged islands. It *is* fair that he is dead. He is at least beyond the daily mortification of having a passionless wife, beyond the defeat of my unbelief, the waste of my uncharity. It is I who am, after all, dead. He is at rest. I have really been dead for a very long time. This that I walk about in is a cold clay case."

She walked no further but sat in a wooden alcove, just aware of pelvic stiffness.

"Incipient arthritis," her mind went on. There was no anxiety. "Inherited tendency. It invades more rapidly when the wish to live is absent."

The last prefects had left the field.

"Along the corridors I see them looking at me, these untried girls who have come here—Julia would triumph to hear it said—to have the clamps of dogma tightened about their already straitened thinking. So it was with me; long, long ago, at the very spring the stream was choked never to find a life-broad flow. Only last Sunday I heard Mother Evangeline giving them the weekly Adult Talk: 'Always sit upright in the chair. Never, never lean back in a relaxed manner. A man, seeing you like that, will be bound to have evil thoughts.' And each listening girl instinctively tightens muscles; braces herself afresh against the assault of man, the enemy. Of course later they will laugh—maybe. Silly old Mother Evangeline, they may say. Rubbish, they may think they think. But a poison, nevertheless, stays deep in the centre. It has already done its work to which no intellectualisation can be antidote. That poison was in fact lodged in them already before they came here and Mother Evangeline has added only a probably unnecessary booster to the earlier innoculation against innocent delight in the flesh.

It is well that Alec is gone. Indeed I coldly killed him. Crime of frigidity. I see them looking at me, these gullible girls, wondering at my face. I have at last perfected the mask; its smiling ice is permanent. It pleases me to see the recoil in their faces.

Soon the nuns' bell will ring. I will go to the mechanical prayer, kneel in my stall, the veil hiding my silence. Despising the cant. No word of it all makes me feel less cold. The routine, the order, the cleanliness of this place please me. Four pleasures: the Dingle girls talking Irish and these. But altogether I have five.

There were other things I could have done. Turned to drink. The end is public, shameful. Everyone knows your sottish end. Privacy is a last necessity. Drugs? Worse than drink. More degrading, more confessedly selfish. And I never had money. Taken the offering lovers? And grown daily more dependent, more fearful because older. None of them would have borne with me as did Alec. I could have held no lover; I had nothing to give.

I considered these things. I found no further hold in the outside world. In latter years my inclination had been more and more to retreat. I considered much. Once, they had wanted me here and I would not stay. Eager then, the insidious blights as yet unfelt, I went into the world to breed many years' puzzlements, confusion; and then knew myself barren. Then having lost any further urge to outwardness, I remembered back to this retreat, a place to wait detachedly for the end I had not the courage to make immediate.

I still possessed the things they once wanted from me here, brain, energy—which even if reduced could still be willed to efficient activity. The inner grave of no-belief was coldly secret, inaccessible to priest or mother superior. Confession? Profession of fervency? They did not bother me. I could now tell sinless lies, who had long striven to live to unattainable truth.

It was not difficult to be accepted here. I was a prodigal returned. They were ready to forgive my humble heart and were unsuspicious of deceit. They were glad to refuge the erring widow whose family was fledged and provided for. Had she not also skills they could use, keeping in the convent useful money? They embraced my edifying vocation.

I have felt relief in the changeless days. So then I practised the smile that very soon became a reflex to the rising bell. Now it serves me most usefully. When they speak to me and I am not disposed to conversation, I merely continue to smile and bow my head and pass along. Everyone respects my reserve. I am the widow who has known much sorrow. They forgive my eccentricity.

Only when I play the organ—the fifth pleasure —a slow forgotten warmth sometimes stirs in me, and in the darkened chapel I know my smile is gone and I feel a wetness on my cheeks.

Contrasts

Goodman was ready to go downstairs and try his luck with the breakfast hazards. He wondered would they be worse than usual this morning. Beatrice had to be soon at the airport and there was all that usual racket of getting ready for school to be handled. But of course Martha had come; the fact of his sister having been installed since last night might help towards smoother running. He didn't know. They got on well enough for two women, Beatrice and herself. Breakfast *might* be a more likely matter. But it wasn't so much a matter of Beatrice handing over to firmer management: now that everything had been decided she would probably be attuned to ceding matters to her sister-in-law from first thing to-day; but she was still vulnerable to the pack. While she was still around they would snap and bark, savaging her attention to the last. Even poor Alice who, from her deaf isolation, had her own irrefutable ways of engaging her mother. Yes, with Martha finally in sole command things would be civilised; anyway more civilised. If chillier. He began to move along from the door of the room.

"Dad," from the annex to the left.

"Yes, what?" Two words much containing. O loving parent be bright, responsive to your depending young first thing in the day. Yes, what?—reflecting inside their meaningful limits something of fifteen years' fathering. Parent by conviction rather than disposition, he had been convinced several times, even twice after they knew about Alice. Or so it would appear. Truth was they had not all been intended but once they were there he did his heart-searching, convinced best by them.

"Dad?"

"I said yes, what?" You don't have your foot outside the bedroom door before they start. You haven't even got up when they are at it. They can start in the dead of night.

"When you are going by, chuck in my school-case will you?"

He chucked. "And what do you want it for?" But he didn't wait for an answer. "You should be up, have eaten by now. It's all hours, school time already." An every-morning reflex of admonishment. He was going down the stairs. Some entanglement in the kitchen. Keep on; brave it.

Martha, rigid, guarded his fruit-juice from a flying dollop of porridge. He could see there was passable progress in preparations except for the two belting one another with porridge spoons. Alice, apart and a little lost of face, was already getting into her coat. Goodman sat down and patiently took the baby's foot, high-chair scope, out of his plate. He was a nice baby. In Goodman's convinced acceptance he assessed the baby as

40

ultimately nice. But sticky, dominating, time-using. Following the family pattern.

His wife was cleaning up the porridge pair at the sink, confining herself to you are dreadfully naughty. She meant to leave as forbearing an aura as possible. She might be gone a month.

Soon the goodbyes echoed. Goodbye my children. Scattering through the door, gaberdine, serge, and bottle-green. Disarray, except for the one tidy one. And *she* was like her mother's conscience, censuring the slipshod. Why isn't this done Mummy, and this? Or, Why is it done that way and not the other? Clean, shining, made for an order of life not theirs. My repudiated convent regimentation reincarnate, her mother would reflect.

Years and years Beatrice Goodman had been coming to the door to say schooltime goodbyes. Every two or three years an extra child was added to the car. She would stand and watch them being driven off by Goodman until the trees at the bend hid the car, waving all the time. Before they went there was always a departure kiss. Mostly the small ones came to meet her halfway with it but sometimes refused her, knowing the value of refusal: she had hurt their heads getting tangles out; she had dried faces too brusquely; their breakfast drink had been too hot and had scalded their mouths, or something like this. Always the holding-back was a punishment for her someway shortcomings. While she might still be bent over a small head registering in swift reaction the individual smell of young hair and skin, the older ones, rushing past, might plant on the side of her face, her ear, or any handy top part, their kiss, their pledge of careless bond somewhere in the complexity of adolescence. If they passed without doing this she knew something more than hurry was the matter: she had failed also in some way towards them or they were suffering some knot. She would stay on the doorstep after they had gone, wondering what it was this time, regardless of her motley: graceless dressing-gown, demented hair, flittered night-dress—never time to mend her own things. For a moment she would stay, for ten or five, depending on her mood, the weather or the relative urgency of the current baby's needs.

To-day Alice had delayed around her; the porridge pair grudged kissing and stomped in injury and accusation. Because she was going away. She had tried telling them, with cajolery, with self-justification, during the previous week. No use. The going away, much-needed holiday or no, they took, so far, only as an offence, a betrayal. They did not want Martha as substitute. Their aunt, salt of the earth, model of rectitude, deserted by a gay-boy husband—none of which they realised—was very particular, which they realised very well. She had no children, an immaculate routine and house. Had she had any children they would also doubtless be routined immaculately. In Martha there was little fulfilled give. One part of Beatrice had qualms at leaving the family to her; another said: It'll do them all good, not least Martha who is dying to show she can make a better hand of things than me. I'll be, maybe, better valued when I get back. She had worked herself dry trying to get everything in the place ready for her absence but she knew her best, limited by all severe pressures, would be far short of Martha's standards. Anyway, everything now had been agreed on. The doctor had said. Goodman had said. He had also said she'd come back with the edges rounded a bit. Not that he put it that way to the family. "Your Mummy needs a change. She'll be all the nicer Mummy when she gets back." Babying the talk, hiding feeling.

She turned from the door and hurried through the hall. Time was short. To-day she was not going to ponder on anyone's wounds. In her mind she was harsh with misgiving and, on realising it, was harsher still against examining it. She would not even glance at any personal unease but would push all troubling down under the frantic hour between now and getting on the plane. She might later try to sort out on the flight. At the moment she was feeling no holiday anticipation and could not imagine it possessing her to cancel out anxieties. As she ticked off the last of her packing list she was trembling. Over the past week in spite of non-inclination, she had, with detachment, done some work on her clothes. In the very early hours of that morning she had carefully packed most of them; it was the only time out of the twenty-four she counted as being almost free from family demands. Even then the baby could have awakened. When she got into bed, cold, Goodman grumbled a little and then awake enough to realise the reason for her lateness and disturbing chill, patted her sleepily: "Husbands divorce for less. But I'll forgive you. Have a good time woman . . . let it be . . . a rest." He was asleep on the last word. He needed rest badly himself.

Without actually looking she absently noticed herself a few times in the long mirror before which was propped her case. Once she stopped a full minute to regard herself distantly, removedly. She coldly concluded she was a pitiable enough object: hair crazy; worried face; bag of a dressing-gown. She bitterly decided that when she got away she would buy a fetching negligée no matter what. In Eve's central heating she could be diaphanous with impunity. But just now apart from the bitter decision, in itself part clear-cut countering defiance against her confused condition, she didn't care how she would look, couldn't imagine how she would care. With a final inclusive disparagement of her dilapidated self she turned from the mirror. Goodman doesn't see me anymore. He just *knows* me. I only need to dress up, put up a front, for those who only see me. In the next few weeks I'll have to put up some show. Maybe I'll feel more like that too, later. Kids . . . Alice, oh poor Alice . . . and chores left to one side, who knows . . . ?

While she delayed a moment to smell the soap Goodman had bought for her—small gestures he made, minor extravagances conveying mixed wealth—she heard the baby crying downstairs. Was Martha, drilled Beatrice-wise for a solid hour last night, doing the right things, the Beatrice-things by the baby? More than likely not. Martha thought she knew children; she was active in the S.P.C.C. and other such bodies that gave her a vicarious satisfaction as an imagined mother, righteous and virtue-spreading. Martha is a straight decent woman, Beatrice Goodman. Yes, but her secondhand state is undeviating from rule of rote. And that being so, what then are you doing going away? Won't your child show some terrible later repercussions? Shh worry; worry only begets more. You *are* going. You must be ready soon. It *is* trojan of Martha to take over. How grateful you should be. And it's true you are fagged out. A wreck really. Maybe you will be able to enjoy. If once you can let go.

She briefly smelled the expensive soap, realising its authentic perfume. Later I will appreciate it better maybe—if once I get in a perfume mood. She was remembering the smell of young hair and cheeks just kissed and was troubled in spite of harsh resolving by accusing eyes and bony knees and hair badly brushed for school. I'll go down in history as a neglectful mother and that isn't fair. I have worked hard. Desperately hard. Self-pity. She was crying shaking on the new talc that went with the soap and, smelling nothing at all, she shoved soap and talc into their shiny wallet and closed her case lid down on top of them.

It was an out of context procedure driving to the airport, dressed in a mechanical determined best, face at least cursorily made-up, all by ten o'clock. This time any other morning she would be in the thick of chores. It was altogether too soon to be relaxed. She was struggling with pushing responsibility into an impossible non-existence. What was the use of its unescapable weight since it was now a futile, an impotent quantity.

"Tell Martha—oh how could I have forgotten this—that the baby . . ." But Goodman gripped her knee. "She's not a fool, Beatrice. Now it'll be all right, fine. Just take it easy woman. Let yourself have some fun. We'll *miss* you but . . . enjoy it."

"It would be so much better if you could come with me." She meant it and the next second was doubtful whether she did. She could not scrutinise what was in her mind. Three years since she had been alone anywhere.

Only minutes to spare as they climbed to the departure gates. When her flight number was called they looked into each other's faces seeing each a face deeply known, that each had hurt, goaded, hated, with the hate that is of love. A thing to be wondered at, their need of one another. They did

45

not acknowledge tears. He laughed in little coughs and, holding her shoulders, shook her.

"Just a few weeks," he said, "a little while."

"Yes." And then they were moving in different directions.

Once arrived at the terminal the need for independent action stirred her to a more positive level. Up to this point since she had left Goodman the smooth conveyor-belt services had left her free to brood sunkenly. Now a taxi; flowers for Eve. She would have to brisk up a bit if only out of self-respect; that and the basics of behaviour. Eve hated people to be gloomy: Beatrice, guest, owed brightness to Eve, hostess. Mentally checking back, she remembered that last time Eve wore an orange wig and purple eye-shadow, so she bought orange and purple flowers. Even if Eve had switched since to other colours—a most likely thing—she probably still retained some affection for the previous combination.

"My dear! How *lovely* of you! Just the ones I need."

The place was full of flowers already.

". . . and how . . . well you look. A little *tired* perhaps, but that's to be understood. And we are going to do something about it, mm?"

She showed Beatrice to the usual room where there were additional luxuries since the last time, three years before.

"I do so hope you will be comfortable but let me know if there is anything . . ."

It would be impossible to improve on what she was getting, Beatrice thought, and then in spite of some blunt pride, said it, because Eve had always been so generous: come for as long as you like only entertain yourself. The arrangement had been like this over many years. Here's your key and do exactly as you want. Eve, as hostess, could hardly be better. "There will be the odd friends as always you know, Bee, a party or so as always . . . but maybe you'll be too tired . . . ?" "No, no, I won't be; I'm already much less tired." It was not just a reflexive banality of fitting-in that made her answer so. She was, indeed, already a little less taut in direct response to the diametric difference between Eve's mellifluous ethos and the unending urgencies in the air at home. This response brought its own small train of guilt. Thou art faithless. Traitress.

"Dave is coming to tea."

Her stepson. Twice married and divorced, Eve at the moment was probably between husbands. But almost certainly not manless. She was never that.

"Dave dying to see you again."

Hardly so but let it pass. Dave, languid, epicurean, well-legacied, shrewdly-invested, *might* die of sudden reality did his income somehow suddenly get cut off.

"And how are the darling children?"

Eve knew only the off-duty side of her visitor, having resisted, but charmingly, all invitations to the proliferating centre. Beatrice knew she dreaded the avalanche of young but it would be unthinkable for Eve to couch refusal in any brutal plainness. Her wording was always carefully plausible. Eve, of easy sophistication and sanguine enquiry, truly preferred children, at any level, in small measure. So briefly, not to bore, Beatrice answered. She kept herself braced doing it because answering meant imminent threat from bony knees and lost deaf eyes. Already begun to be lulled a little in the new aura, an anaesthesia of flowers, warmth, orderliness, childlessness, she even resented Eve's asking, the replying necessity of touching on realities so only barely filmed. But Eve was civilised: such enquiry was as much part of her as her ultra style.

Dave, modishly shabby, did come, bringing with him a man in multi-striped trousers.

"Boncho darling, what marvellous trousers!"

"Yawh, yesterday Portobello Road."

He lay down at Beatrice's feet. Maybe my ankles aren't swollen today? I haven't been doing any standing. Why the devil should I care. He's weird. But she cared. Bag of a dressing-gown a world away. Goodman just knows me. Boncho is looking at my legs.

Boncho had brought a cake. "Thought you'd be having tea round about now." From the floor he threw it up to Eve. Uncalled-for hysterics from Eve: "Boncho darling, you really are quite something." Beatrice wondered. It couldn't be, or then again could it? Eve had fairly catholic tastes.

He was up again straddling an oak bench and treating a mug of tea to some control. Holding a hand flat over the top of the mug he squeezed it in spasms round the middle with the other. Through a chink in his fingers he inspected the contents, considering and grim. He took a sampling sip without relish and contrarily followed up by swallowing the whole scalding lot in one go after which he gave Beatrice an ear to ear smile. Absolute bonkers. Eve urged him to some of his cake. He waved her off in seeming affliction.

"Beatrice, how is the complex?" Dave always referred to her family in this way. He was parading with his mug, making loud drinking noises. He customarily made use of different perverse ploys to offset elegance. Does he really want an answer?

Test the gambit. "Dead, Dave, they are all very dead." "Good," he said. And so it is tested. "Won't you, Beatrice, have some of this—rustic wheat? I go for it." He didn't want an answer either to that. He was occupied in untidy bread, heavy with butter. His arrangement. This rustic leaning was a new ploy.

"Hm, I go for it too," Boncho said. He began to hack off his own lump and hunked on butter. He ate in a big hurry until it was finished, by which time his jaws had a buttery gleam. Eve held out a napkin to him. He ignored it and deliberately wiped his face with his hand and his hand on the stripes. Then he plummetted again to Beatrice's feet and waved a finger at her: "God was my grandfather." He was solemn about this.

"How nice for you." She could think of nothing clever.

"How extra nice for me." He gave no evidence of pleasure. "God is a Jew. My name is Solomons."

"Boncho is my treasurer." A shuttling of purple eyelids. Dear Eve. She has continued to like purple.

"Eve," Boncho said, "has no head for affairs. I market her pictures."

"A jewel. A treasure. A treasurer." Eve tinkled the lightest laugh having said it.

"Feeble dahling," Dave remarked without acrimony.

"Why can't Beatrice come to see my studio?" asked Boncho Solomons. His hand on her ankle as he began to get up. Need for balance. There was also handy a heavy chair-leg which he did not avail of. "Eve, bring her up, up, under the glass top."

"Why not indeed!" Eve was a nuance too ready? "Why not let's cook dinner up at your place? I just got two Chateau Pontet Canet. Let's break them in, mm?"

"Absolutely."

Boncho's studio was at the top of Eve's flat-block. They took up the two bottles of wine and Dave and Eve cooked while Boncho Solomons sketched his lightning impression of the earth mother and that was Beatrice Goodman. She saw herself projected as a wall-length headless creature whose one enormous foot and swollen ankle grew out of her neck and whose three confineless faces were poised one over the liver, one in the groin, and one staring in astonishment up from where the transposed foot should be. Down her left side she wore fifteen variegated breasts and on the right, at knee-level, a single mountainous nippled bulb.

"Chi, chi," breathed Eve, bringing a tureen to stir before the mural. "He got nine hundred clear for the last *Fecund Primitive* but since I was the model it had only, let me see, one, two, three—" she was counting down the breasty side "—mine had only eight, *and* there was no birth symbol." She centred with a long lovely finger on the face in the groin. "Of course I never did give birth did I? Boncho had to strain his imagination. But this, this is *generous*, really. I mean all senses of the word you know. Really yes. Boncho darling! worked on a little this should fetch the even thousand."

Eve is brave. She deserves better by now. Easy, not so snap; you can't really decide about him yet; to be fair you must wait to see more what he's made of.

"I will not take less than a thousand," said Boncho, dumping a small roasted bird—it might have been a snipe—on his plate.

Later Beatrice Goodman took a bath in Eve's ochre and red bathroom. It only wakened her up.

It might have been partly the colours, but she could not sleep that first night. Let it be a—rest. Goodnight Goodman. A world away. I cannot sleep.

Mistress Of The Junket

It was a pity Julian Alderton had ever come across that pacifist fellow, Riordan, so all his family thought. From the time he met him he began to change for the worse, they one and all agreed. When he left the army like that they said it was appalling what putty he was in Riordan's hands. Apart from spending all available time with the man when he came on those lecture-tours to England, Julian, it would appear, was subject to remote control from him as well. That was why he had gone out of the army. A hypnotised act. The Aldertons had seen Riordan on television: they liked neither the way he looked nor what he said. His socks were in Argyle check and when he delivered himself of his egalitarian heresies he doubly offended with an unspeakable accent.

Had Julian remained in the army, they were quite convinced, he would have got quickly to the top through one connection and another: they had influential ties and Julian could be a sticker at a thing once his mind was made up. But his mind, now, seemed radically turned from the true course and made up in all the wrong directions. His revelation of untraditional sentiments was grievously distressing; his decision to search out work in Ireland, where Riordan lived most of the time, was renegade. He left England soon after this decision and thenceforward there seemed only decreasing hope of salvaging him from lowering influences.

"Ireland, of course," Mrs. Alderton would say to the other proper-minded members of the family, "does have its proportion of the right sort of people but Julian just does not seem to set any store by them. Once—how sadly far away it seems—he was as . . . discriminating, as anyone else of his blood. More so even; at that time one could have said he was, indeed, a snob."

From Ireland he wrote faithfully to his mother she being the only one of his aggregate family as regular, as reciprocal as he in that respect. She duly relayed to the rest the latest strange thinking detailed in his letters. He continued to protest and argue the rightness of his outlook. It was in exact alignment with Riordan's, a fact which Julian, less than tactful in his crusading procedure, underlined. The Aldertons never allowed a moment's tolerance of his postulated ethic. They could scarcely imagine other than that he was slightly mad.

His subsequent behaviour did nothing to diminish this imagining. However, the family, his mother excepted, were not concerned for his sake. They worried only as to how explain him without losing face with their friends and relatives. They were well and widely connected and their inherited values were sacrosanct. Loss of face because of Julian's defection did certainly worry his mother but she was also truly concerned for what she conceived to be her son's well-being: he appeared to have plunged himself irretrievably into penury and anonymity. Riordan seemed to be peculiarly addicted to social work and Julian gave all available time now to the same sort of thing.

"One understands, of course, that such people exist, are all around; one sees them if one so chooses but one does not have to *know* them. One has the right to pick, select one's friends and acquaintances. Not that there were not other Aldertons, past and present, who had had a turn at ameliorating the oddities and poverties of the lowborn." Mrs. Alderton was, however, careful to emphasise that those others, those Aldertons who so properly belonged to the gaitered, buttressed establishment of God on earth, the Church of England, had acted acceptably containing their altruistic operations at a proper distance, not once forgetting their own privileged rating, nor once had they been so unbalanced as to see the objects of their impeccable charity as there but for the grace of Fortune go we. In their measured ministrations towards the flotsam and jetsam, nothing had suggested to their admirable dispositions curious notions about accidents of birth. Julian—and it was of course that man, Riordan, undermining sanity with freakish experiments, who was to blame—did not so contain himself. He mingled, entertained, holidayed all within the masses. He identified with them. This last debased process was particularly deplorable, indicating a disturbing emotional looseness.

When he had first written of his intention to marry they asked with little hope "*Who* is she? Is she *one of us* or does she belong to the *lower orders*?" with this necessary stress. Had she been Anglo-Irish there might have been some traceable blood-link with relics of the Ascendancy. From his replies they deciphered that she was bog-Irish—her name was Siobhán, unpronounceable—and a member of the Roman Church, poor, obscure, one remove from peasant. Her grandparents on both sides had been mountain farmers. Her great wealth, he had written, was a natural vigour of mind and body. He was immensely proud of her innate "glow" and much taken by the fact that her kind of education had left her unspoilt, innocent—one could readily envisage the ghastly raw schools, the rudimentary convents anchored in medieval ignorance. Clearly an outsider! Julian's further deviation from tradition in marrying such a girl was a confirmation of his crazing condition.

As if this were not sufficient he proceeded to engender a family without any of the financial equipment which one simply must have. A debasing of the ancestral blood in one hybrid was painful enough to consider but he did not remain content with one mixture. Nor two. Nor three. It seemed as if he might, with this heavy-hipped peasant, continue to reproduce indefinitely. It was quite horrible.

"Like mice and rabbits. It is too low of him to cite the Victorians and Greatmamma. One cannot possibly have even the most basic decencies with more than two children nowadays, not in these changed times when servants are just too outrageously expensive and one is getting no return for one's money—one is dreadfully reluctant to give thought to the squalor in which Julian and his proliferant brood must wallow."

Julian brought the Irish girl to his mother's

London home one bleak winter when she was engorging with some pregnancy—". . . one cannot keep tally, one prefers not to count. One longs to understand. One would wish to use this winter-time visit to fullest benefit but does not quite know how to approach the intractable divisive territory. An impossible diplomacy is called for. It has been really too altogether . . . upsetting, of Julian to have been so very . . . awkward . . . not to have married someone more congruously-born." But the visit was marked, particularly, in its early part, by a level of seemly outward behaviour. Decorum was the keynote. All the immediate relatives in due rota came to the house for the purpose of meeting Siobhán Alderton—". . . how oddly the names combine!" Well-bred, anonymous conversation with the new accretion was achieved —and private extended comment throve.

"True, the quality of the voice is soft but the accent is such as has not been heard anywhere before: it is not even West British, is it?"

"Quite. It is undeniable that her appearance is enormously healthy. Incredibly fertile-making."

At that point someone remembered about Toppington's young mare.

"Too very bad indeed that the dear little mare should have to be put down the other day when she was so near. She and the unborn foal—what a dreadful loss to poor Toppy! He had simply adored that fragile animal. Unfortunate, unfair, how delicate these matters of health and reproduction are, with thoroughbreds."

"Pregnancy does so interfere with the hang."

"Hang?"

"Of a garment. Don't you agree?"

"Ah yes. Julian's wife—do say her name again,

my dear, you are so good at it—yes, yes, that's it —how curiously it is spelt then!—Well, *she* has spoken of the amount of time her sewing takes from her reading. Undoubtedly her industry is admirable, and she may be quite excellent at making things for her children, but she appears to have allowed no time to make anything for herself. One single maternity garment is scarcely sufficient—not for the needs of the present visit at any rate."

The new Mrs. Alderton's unequal demeanour presented difficulties; diffidence and too-sensitive front were plain signs of inferiority-feeling about which simply nothing could be done. Her spurts of brashness which might have been ineffectual efforts to establish some identity in an area of elusive codes, of invisible gauges, were seen as regrettably common. Her conversation could be admitted to be intelligent but the subjects she veered towards —social justice, experimental living and suchlike insubstantial abstractions—were scarcely appropriate, and, while one agreed she was mentally agile, one felt (with the assurance of unimpeachable lineage) that the virtuosity of brainflights was not required: one was left unimpressed by what she might believe to be her mental advantage. Her only other advantage, natural health, they met as an embarrassing testimony of her stout peasant blood. They, all of them, rested carefully every single afternoon and before any social sortie.

Julian and Siobhán had brought one small child with them on the visit. From their handling of him one needed very little effort to picture the mores obtaining amongst the other products of their union who were at a fortunate distance in Ireland. For a person of his class Julian Alderton had the oddest approaches to upbringing. In the first place he believed his wife should herself see to the child's wants.

"The practice of having a nanny take over a mother's most intimate dealings with her child is in every way deleterious to the tender life," he pronounced to his mother and assembled relatives. "Children," he expanded, "should be as free-growing plants that, nurtured generously and proportionately in all their parts, will flower in unblighted beauty."

"You, yourself, were attended to, not only by Nanny, but by two nursery-maids—always," his mother said, as one in pain.

"It is not necessary to remind me. You don't imagine I forget, do you? Notice my unblighted beauty."

"That is ridiculous Julian. I do insist that you all, as a family, profited very much by the fact that I dealt only with the more predictable aspects of you as children and that I left your quite too frightening tantrums to Nanny."

"You were a conscientious mother in the light of your class and times. I really do understand very well that you were most zealous in the observances of your kind." Julian's voice as he said this had the constraint of someone who fears the possible uncontrol of feeling. As a child it had been a matter for wonder how he worshipped his mother. His present attitude seemed to indicate a wishful forgiveness of the flawed system that had organised his vulnerable years; only the family seemed disposed to see his intimations as yet another witness to eccentricity. His forgiveness was superfluous where they were concerned since they saw no reason to be absolved by him. That he was humble, wanting to be forgiven himself for what they might consider remiss in him, made no difference at all to them. How could one forgive when the defaulter persisted in his faults? To persist in his way of life, to continue endeavours at justification, this was intransigence apparently not to be overlooked. It could have been that understanding was what Julian most needed from his people: he appeared to be quite beyond their understanding. Undeniably his mother had her own very particular brand of feeling for him but some of its manifestations were uncommonly like the symptoms of a proprietary conditional affection. In the third week of their stay he could be heard speaking to Siobhán, somewhat sadly, about the intractable area between his mother and himself.

"Unconditional love," he generalised at the finish, "is what the human race needs."

"There is no such thing and it is a hopeless need."

"It is the sort of love I give you," he said and she did not disagree. They had been married almost a decade during which time most forces relating to their situation—inherent in it and external to it —could be said to have acted against their initial bond; yet it had held and he was still with her, agonisingly earnest in avowal of faithfulness to her, to their unrewarding circumstances. After some thought she said, "I believe you. But I think I really like only my children in this unconditional way, and they are extensions of myself. So I do not progress from myself really."

The child did not blossom appreciably in the ethos of Mrs. Alderton's house. Native spontaneity was likely to meet the implacable resistance of a certain shape of smile, to find itself limited by innumerable edicts, expressed or implicit, but unmistakable as manacles of iron. Juxtaposed to adults other than his parents, he was liable to be curtailed by judgements emanating from under-spoken fronts.

Julian and his wife were increasingly exercised to temper with extreme care whatever influences bore on their child. Their earnestness kept them short of humour, and not infrequently as the visit progressed their seriousness tended to terseness with each other, to airs of injury and even open breach. Believing a presentation of parental harmony essential for a child's stability, they managed to keep their arguments for the night, when their child slept; to this degree they were in control of their relationship. But they were sleeping poorly. In the wakeful times Siobhán dwelt broodingly on cankering matters; she muttered heavily into the dark about disparities from roots up between her and Julian's family.

"The differences are like oil and water. I am being silently shouted inferior and I know myself equal. Even better. It is useless to attempt any breakthrough. Anything I say about the merits of brains over inherited position, about the necessity for a classless society—anything—is heard merely as callow evidence of my inner inadequacy. I find myself being managed. There are agile diplomacies at work to timetable the child, to dictate the method of his feeding, the arrangement of his appearance." She mimicked Julian's mother: "A lovely lovely bath is now ready for the little thing, a lovely lovely bath with *such* a sweet little duck to share the water." She stopped and heaved her swollen shape unhappily. "That duck," she went on, "was bought by your mother with mixed motives, and so was the spoon-and-pusher." She took on Mrs. Alderton's tone again. "Just imagine, I found the sweetest little spoon-and-pusher for our baby. You will remember Julian how Nanny always found it such a help: our baby will be able to eat nicely now by himself."

Julian was sitting upright in the chilly dark, remaining silent. "She bought the young fellow a beautiful new outfit also don't forget," he, at length, countered Siobhán.

"Yes, agreed it is splendid quality. But it is an implied slur on the clothes I myself so carefully prepared for him before leaving Ireland. It is unbelievable how much they consider 'vulgar'. I'm made to feel in the subtlest way that the clothes I put together do not meet the grade. Even if you, Julian, have rejected such petti-fogging trivia, she—they—all of them, are rigidly ruled by their minutiae of stupid values that stamp a body as not belonging."

Emotion got the better of her. Forgetting that the child was not to be wakened she ranted at Julian:

"You have betrayed me, bringing me here. You should not have submitted me, defenceless, in my poor clothes, my ignorance of their sort of idiotic fine points, to the silent knives, to this Arctic ordeal. What is most defeating of all is that these Aldertons are devoid of any truly finer apprehensions, incapable of any exploring, enlightening discussion. Their thinking is effete, contracted, stultified, closed to the real worth of individuals."

Julian refuted nothing. "We are to leave pretty soon. It is not really a fundamental issue that things be different here, that the family attitudes change. They won't. By our sticking together through thick and thin we have established the important issue. We—you, I, the children—are representatives of the vital fusion. We have incarnated the newer way. And since it is not a vital matter what they think here, you must keep faith and accept."

"I don't quite know what that means," she said. "No, I do not accept."

"It means that you are you: your essential self is inviolable." To this she did not reply and they went into a wounded sleep.

The following morning Julian fell ill, there, in his mother's house; the visible tokens were those of 'flu; for days his eyes wept and wept. His mother appeared intensely concerned. She cooked—she was a superlative cook—countless little delicacies to cosset his appetite. He would sit blearily amongst his pillows being spooned into and saying "My dear mother is a mistress of the junket; she was always such a marvel with invalid food. I had forgotten how marvellous . . . her food could taste."

His wife, witnessing what could pass for regressive relish, might have found the eulogy ambiguous: an endorsement of his mother's art by implied detraction from hers, an addition of his slight to those of all the others. She left his convalescence to his mother and, taking the child, went to stay with some Irish friends in another part of London: ebullient people at whom Mrs. Alderton, should she ever have to meet them, might smile with an annihilation of propriety and ice. Siobhán and Julian were to have visited them the day he fell ill, and her departure to them now, at this point, was open to arbitrary interpretation.

In this new area at first she gave all signs of rejoicing in the easy ways of her friends, their relaxed speech, habits of eating, their dislike of formality. But in a while something like a blight suggested itself in her and appeared to spread taking the form, after a couple of days, of a restraint towards her friends. Once in her room when the child had gone to sleep she cried out "O horrible thing that is happening to me . . . I begin to devalue my own people, I begin to see them as might my mother-in-law." When she next mingled with them she evinced especial deference and obligingness.

Once only she rang up the Alderton home to inquire after Julian and her voice came calm, remotely cool. He was much improved, she learned, had been up, but was now taking a nap. She capped each meticulous, strained sentence of Mrs. Alderton's with a deliberate, artificial "Really?", "Imagine!" or "How splendid!". There seemed something of triumph in her as she put down the phone. "I am mastering the expedient game quite suddenly," she said to the room packed randomly with chainstore bargains, the prized purchases of her hardworking friends.

"I love your room," she called down the stairs to one of her friends ascending, and her voice had a tone quite other than that which she had used to Mrs. Alderton. "O joy, O room, O people," she sang and the friend looked at her unsurely, then passed on saying: "You're hard to make head or tail of these days, Siobhán."

The next day Siobhán dressed the child in the favoured clothes she had made him and, having bestowed warm blessings on her friends, took him off in a taxi to her mother-in-law's house. "You have been so wonderful getting Julian on his feet again," she told Mrs. Alderton with a skimming airiness, and Julian, depleted, seemed less than easy before the evidence of this urbane armour. In his drained state he could have been perturbed at what it signified of likely offensive and consequent further emotional demand on himself. He could be noticed remaining a few moments in a deep stillness, his eyes closed. When he opened them a returning strength announced itself in his face and continued distinctly to advance in his general mien while he firmly arranged matters for departure. Not very long afterwards he, his wife and child were ready for the boat train. Several of the relatives collected for tempered farewells. Siobhán made an inclusive gesture saying: "My stay with you all has been of immense benefit to me" and she smiled with that light air noticeable in her only since her return; she said it as though investing them with a favour. Julian said: "We have—all—a long way to travel."

As the taxi drove away Mrs. Alderton might have been freshly assailed with thoughts of Riordan. Her glasses were clouded but she did nothing about them until quite some minutes later when the small concourse dissolved, becoming absorbed into various nooks of afternoon retirement.

The Tree

She had come alone to think about the tree. Its fruit was growing again and now it was November.

Below her was the seaweed, massed in interminable tangle, brown, black, beautiful. Uncountable relating shapes. The tide was out and it was November.

Away on the left lay the city, seeming remote because of a bluish fog about the general mass of it. A few erections, the Power House, the gasometer, she could identify; and a few others she did not recognise nor did this matter at all to her. She looked and saw much that she did not see.

Now and then people walked along the sea-terrace dressed for the high wind and spattering sharp rain that did not yet come steadily. They were, she thought, mostly settled, local people, walking off heavy Sunday lunches. Some who passed were, however, young: in their teens or early twenties. Vinyl coats, long scarves, knitted hats pulled down over ears. Their hair blew with flying scarf tails. She wondered peripherally about them while yet the tree was most in her mind. Had *they* eaten yet? Would they go back to some room together and cook while the rain came heavily? Had they slept together yet? Would they later gather with others and smoke pot?

She went down steps towards the rippled sand, not wishing to notice limp sweet-papers and other ugliness of rubbish, marking the tide line along the base of the sea wall. There was much less flotsam now than in the summertime but she preferred to look beyond.

Four ships equally distanced from one another were on the farther reaches of the water. Behind them rose a flat-topped hill. The ships had not moved since she had come; she remembered the dock-strike: they would stay there indefinitely.

Nobody, it had seemed, had wanted to know about the tree. She would have liked to have shown its fruit. Nobody had seemed interested that she had kept alive the inconspicuous dwarf tree that bore peculiar fruit.

She could not remember ever having been without it; always it had been hers; always she had moved it wherever she had moved, lifting it in the dark and planting it again in the dark, remembering to nourish it a little every now and then. Always it grew as before, never reaching beyond a certain height.

The fact of its living related to undefined areas in her, the way breathing related to her physical self. To breathing she gave scarcely the slightest conscious attention: should it cease she would die. Yet there were times when she consciously troubled about the dwarf stature of the tree, questioning if this were not, in part, due to the way she always kept it undernourished in a hidden place. It blossomed contrarily, a few scattered unimportant blossoms that were not seen except by her. Sometimes the blossoms shrivelled and there was then no small harvest. Those times she wept telling tears to no one.

On the rare times when fruit developed she picked it, and, as she stayed in the shadows, wondered at the strangeness of it; at its persistence in growing and swelling to a painful fulness against discouragement.

Langley, and a few others, were aware a little, and at a distance, of her involvement with the existence of the tree. Occasionally they remarked that this was a species that more should be heard of, and then they moved away, busy about their different things. They did not know that sometimes she felt hopeless about the failure of the crop; despairing because she could neither disengage herself from the life of the tree nor forgive her inadequacy in nourishing it: to other shortcomings in herself she was merciful. Its life having a significance for her which she did not understand, it could not therefore be explained by her to anyone. Nor did she try an explanation. Such dwelling on intangibles might be considered egocentric indulgence.

Had Langley and the others known her strange despair, they would have spoken many kind platitudes for her comfort. These she did not wish to hear. Platitudes irritated her; the mode of their utterance was usually such as to make their verity an annoying quantity.

Langley knew people who could have advised her; about fostering growth and what that entailed: knowledge of feeding, pruning, of blight, parasites, atmosphere, fruit promotion. She knew a little about these things herself but not enough and one day she made a decision for a plan of cultivation. Her energy, time, discipline would be dedicated to the working of this plan, which would clarify, after Langley had helped her. She spoke to him of her need for introduction to the knowledgeable people. But he interpreted her need differently from what she had expected; those he brought her to speak with, told her nothing that she had not already known. She had hoped for something very different: advice, which, if followed, would quickly bring the productive harvest she saw in the orchards of the prize-winners. Even more: a metamorphosis of existence for herself that would render shadowy places illuminated.

Langley, confident, believed he was countering her disappointment. "Children are more important," he said, and he gave her children.

They were beautiful children and she cared for them and was so busy with them that, for a long time, it might have seemed she had forgotten the tree, for always, without a pause, she passed the coppice encircling it.

Sometimes, year to year, looking from a high window she might see the sun light up the enclosed fruit, and on those times she would run down and out of the house to where she had seen it glow amidst the thicket—silent, compelling in desertion, indestructible. Her hands would bleed among angry briars and her hair tangle in the clutching barbs of neglect while she stretched and stretched to reach a single perfect shape. When her fingers touched it, they remained a moment, soft and speaking and full of gratitude. Then before she took the fruit her hand would slide to a branch under the tired leaves, some of which had already fallen. Looking down she would see these scattered about the briars and greying thistles. All the time caressing the branch, she would, with her other hand, pick up a few of these leaves, hold them awhile sheltered in her curving palm, smell them and then move her nose down to touch them before carefully putting them back. After, she would go away, taking the single fruit, and store it in her secret place. She usually cried during some part of these things.

For days following this, she would not look from that high window but would talk with her friends of the desirability of routine, efficiency, predictability, as if these were things she knew about very well indeed.

The water was a moving mass of grey whereon little ridges rose and raced and broke to white, before the wind. A northern crowding of clouds, above the flattened hill, was thinned in one place and a concave silver sheened there, from some rare light refraction in the upward layers. The sun was deeply hidden. By now it should be somewhere southwest. The November twilight seemed already to enfold the nebulous city.

The years had crowded one upon the other, charged with occupation and event.

Just by chance she had been at a gathering where there were famous experts. She had not looked for this to happen. Indeed she was not a little overcome to find herself at such close possibilities with them. She could have gone then to one of them, she considered, as, herself, one who knew so little, asking for help. But pride held her: nothing so unutterably boring to the informed as a humbly garrulous female, a woman who piles people under with her bombardment of humble inanities—it would be utterly inane, what she would have to say to them.

Had her tree, its leaves, its blossoms, its fruit ever, even once, been a source of botanical notoriety, been the winner of a single award in any kind of show, such victory would have lent poise to conversational gambit with any single individual of the authorities foregathered. There had however been no such victories; her tree was now so neglected as to be considered a weed by all standards of merit. She was dumb before these people with whom she really wished very much to talk.

What could she say?

"I have a tree . . . a rather unusual tree . . . a neglected tree . . . a tree of great potential . . ."

He—whichever one of the famous she might happen to target—would be bound to look instantly bored; so many people must come to him, expecting him to be fascinated by their thing. She dreaded such a look on a face she spoke to. Or equally, and just as terribly, he might be instantly rude, rudeness being an arbitrarily exercised prerogative of the established. In the event of either reaction she would be paralysed.

Just on the heels of these reflections towards self-containment she, extraordinarily, found herself talking to one of the eminent. He was tall and his breath funnelled down about her face, sickish sour with alcohol, the glass in his hand marking the continuation of a lengthy previous session in some pub.

"I have a tree . . ." she began, taking a little hysterical courage from the hope that his perceptions must surely be dulled.

"Ah my dear," he exhaled, "you certainly have more than that."

He waffled backwards and bumped against someone behind him. "Tom!" he was swivelling the other man around, cigarette in hand, "Tom, she says she has a tree, hahaha . . ."

Tom looked at her. It was clear he did not like what he saw.

"She has more than a tree, Tom? Right?"

Tom, not at all drunk and without pity, knew at once her timorous condition. He would be merciful only to be assured.

"You can have it all." Not wasting a second look on her, he cut abruptly away from them. She felt low as the floor, even though all the time believing entirely in the peculiar quality of her hidden forsaken tree.

The evening went on and as it happened she was taken about to talk with many. Having drunk more than a little herself, she heard her tongue patter ahead of her. She was then, as two people: one, standing aside, critical, disparaging of the other one of her who let her silly wagging tongue utter all the privacies that should have been guarded. They were liking her, the knowledgeable ones—except for a few such as Tom—but not for her tree. She made no headway about that. It was plain that all they said, what promises they made, they would relinquish on the sober morrow. Those whose wives or women were absent, particularly jollied her. When it came to talk of taxis away from the place, she was offered lifts. Yet, oddly, Tom seemed to be the only one going in her direction.

Grudgingly he told her she could be dropped off from his taxi. She wanted to refuse haughtily but, perversely, was drawn on by his churlishness to accept. A rude man though terrifying, perhaps because so, could also be a challenge.

In the taxi, her fatuous tongue, still wilful, independent of an ineffectual restraint too slow inside her, ran on, using the very word with which she grudged to indulge him: he would recognise its indication of his attraction for her.

"You are the terrifying man who has been so hugely successful . . ." He had just become director of his institute.

In the passing street lights she could see the contempt in his face.

"Listen," he said without looking at her, "there is a name for women like you."

Her tongue, suddenly weighted, did not trip again. When she rummaged the rattling fare from her handbag he made no gesture to stop her, no pretence of an intention to pay. Her sudden clear decision not to be obliged to him had been superfluous.

When the taxi stopped outside her door, she let herself quickly out dropping, with a brief defeated relish, what she considered the correct money on the seat beside him. Then she raced up the steps.

She did not tell Langley any of this. He would probably have said something like, "Poor pet, I have warned you often. Don't be upset; you have your children."

She had gone around the rooms looking at their different sleeping shapes.

During the week following, she cut down the tree. She did this when the house was empty and the children sure to be at school still for several hours. She made a great fire, having poured immolating oil all over the uncomplaining branches. She did not stay to watch and she did not go back again.

That had all been some measureless time before.

To-day, while she was in the high room and when she had not, at first, even realised that she was seeing, the sun had again lit up the fruit.

So she had come, alone, to think about the strange miracle of the indestructible tree. She was sad, and ashamed, and full of gratitude.

She lifted her face against the piercing rain and watched the opening clouds beyond the still ships.

Washing Up And
Black Puddings

This night there was a new thing about the tea
wash-up. Minnie put a tin tray on the table when
all the crockery was shoved to the middle for
washing. Kitty had seen the tray being bought
that day in the hardware. They had all been in
Ballyowen and Eily, the cousin on holidays from
working in big English houses, was with them. It
was a church feastday which meant no school but
the Ballyowen shops open all the same. Sheamus,
who would have much preferred to stay at home,
drove them in the pony-trap with a resignation
habitual to these town trips he had to undertake
for family sake.

Always wanting to know the why and wherefore
of everything, Kitty had questioned about the tray
when they were in the hardware but Minnie shut
her up with a fierce undertoned "Conduct yourself."

In front of people not of the family it was
enough. At home she would have gone on pestering
with questions until tempers were lost. Now when

the tray was put down on the table she asked, "What's that for?"

Minnie, in prim simulated surprise, ascended, "For the washing-up, of course."

Kitty understood the "of course" was for the benefit of the cousin, Eily. For some reason her mother wanted the cousin to think the tray was the most usual thing in the world. But Kitty was at home now and not to be satisfied with inadequate information. She spoilt things for her mother by going on, "But we've never had a tray for the wash-up before. What will you do with it?"

"It's to put the wet crockery on," offered Eily.

"What for?"

"To collect the water," said Eily.

"Of course," said Minnie. The most usual thing in the world. Of course.

"But the water always dripped on to the floor before."

Red began to show on the sides and front of Minnie's neck.

"Well, it did," Kitty insisted, in spite of the red warning which she recognised very well. "I never saw a wash-up but there was a pool of water on the floor after it."

"None of your impertinence! Silence!" Censorship. Tactic of the insecure. All Minnie's neck and the tops of her cheeks were red now, her upper lip stretched straight, sign of strain. She was tired and finding it very hard to hold her temper. It would have greatly relieved her to give Kitty a few sound wallops and a rattle of abuse but she wasn't going to do that in front of Eily. If it hadn't been for Eily the whole thing would never have arisen anyway, for all Minnie had wanted was that their domestic procedures might not contrast too primitively with those of the big English houses. Her little expedient refinement with the tray would have been a tiny triumph, a minute inner solace, had it succeeded.

She continued trying to make it succeed by ignoring Kitty: she didn't exist, therefore she couldn't have spoken—and Kitty suffered from the exclusion and was effectively punished by it. She also hated Minnie for it: she had only spoken the truth but her mother would never admit that. Often the mother actually arrived at a point of belief in her own pathetic little pretensions, so necessary were they to her. If this question of the tray and the wash-up were later to be raised between herself and Kitty, she, quite likely by that time, would have convinced herself of her own rightness in the matter.

Jo was watching and listening. No sympathy for his sister though. He was already grimacing his pleasure in her defeat, making derisive small noises from his corner. She pretended not to notice but he knew she saw and heard. It was bitter to her the way he always rejoiced in her defeats with never ever from him a single sign of affection.

Yet *she* could feel pity for *him*. There was the night he was whipped because of the damage to the new wall-clock from Tralee. He was accused of cracking it and his repeated denials were of no avail. Sheamus warned if he did not own up he would be whipped: the father painfully valued that his children be truthful. And whipped Jo was. Kitty was harrowed to see it. There he was, his trousers down; crying, denying; his naked thin white legs, ungainly under the shirt tail, filled her with pity. Although often she had been assuaged by his overthrow in rows with her father, this was too shameful and she could feel no gladness in it. Even if he had broken the glass and, at the time, she thought he probably had. Later, many years later, when they could at last speak to one another in their recognition of mutual affection, he told her that he had not. He told her detachedly, his injury apparently absorbed in the years' passing. They both then fell to considering that Nelly might have been the culprit, might have shifted possible blame by accusing him to Sheamus. They decided it would have been typical of Nelly, who had by this long left the place.

She was about tonight, too, but hadn't witnessed the tray incident. The atmosphere would not have been any pleasanter for Kitty with her there. Nor would Nelly have been on Minnie's side either. She would have enjoyed that the bare truth from Kitty had flustered Minnie. Her contribution to the situation might have been her turkey laugh and it would have been at Minnie for trying to put on airs and at Kitty for being vanquished. No champion of principles, Nelly. Her favours were arbitrary and contrary.

Soon she came in, having been trukking outside with milk-buckets. She sometimes did more of this than was necessary, hoping while she was in Thady's way to start some spark out of him. But not much chance; no give at all in Thady. Anyway, Nelly did not get men easily. Not that she was short of looks, but men shied from her hysterical aggressiveness which was fruit of God knew what. Maybe it sprang from the secret blood of "Old Walrus" as Sheamus, in unusual slyness, sometimes called Nelly's father.

Nelly had, it seemed always been a part of their household: Kitty could never remember her not being there. She made periodic visits to her own family on the other side of the parish and a few times she had taken Kitty in the donkey-car. Old Walrus had glowered from the hearth corner, saying never a word but now and again he spat poisonously, slicing the glowing turf. A long moustache drooled wetly down the sides of his bitter mouth. His wife, a wasted version of Nelly, had yet no domineering in her drained face but her eyes brooded unspoken strangeness. It was not a welcoming house. Evil hung there.

"He's afther dhrivin' in the cows for the fair in the maarnin'," Nelly announced of Thady.

"Did he shut the two gates?" asked Minnie.

"Ye-wisha, don't you know he shut the gates," a mild impatience from Sheamus. He rustled the newspaper a bit and straightened it out, the leaves tremoring tinnily all the time he held them. Jo and Kitty often observed, with mixed sympathy, this slight shake of his; Sheamus was sometimes a butt for their mockery, open or secret, according to what they felt they dared. Minnie belittled him, mercilessly chopped him up in general, but she didn't always go with their doing so. Perhaps because it held up the mirror.

While the scene over the tray had been going on Sheamus had been sitting in his usual nightly place: the sugan-bottomed armchair that was huge and decisively his, its back legs tilted, his feet on the bricks arching above the range, the paper comfortably angled for reading over his knees. In this position he was temporarily refuged from family entanglements and would hold his ground as long as possible, ignoring most goings-on. But the remark about the cattle had caught his ear for they were important to him; they were to be sold, he hoped with profit, the next day.

"He'd have to be an awful gom to leave the gates open." His assertion, nevertheless, contained the doubt that Thady might have been remiss. Maybe he should go himself to check. But he was comfortable at last after the long drive from Ballyowen and he didn't want to stir.

"Well isn't he that too?" very sharp, Minnie. "Don't you know you can't depend on him. You have no choice but to see for yourself."

"Tch tch tch tch," Sheamus gruntled. He lowered his feet from their comfortable height and pushed back the legs of the heavy chair with a horrible grating on the flags. Minnie closed her eyes for a long instant but said nothing—remonstration would have meant further energy spent and she was weary fit to drop. Sheamus cleared his throat of tobacco phlegm from multiple channels, unaware of distaste registering in faces around him. Without stooping his fine height, he lifted the kettle off the range and spat through the circular opening underneath into the fire. Perfect aim. A hiss came from the madly boiling spit and he watched it, a diminishing small ball, dancing itself to nothingness on a fiery sod. He put back the kettle and shuffled off his old slippers to pull on a pair of boots. Then out the backdoor.

"Jo and Kitty, time for you to be going to bed." Kitty's existence was acknowledged again.

"I won't go same time as her," Jo brazened his mother.

"You'll go when you're told. Same time as 'she' —mind your grammar."

"Whichever gets off their shoes the first can stay longer?" Jo was in hope.

Minnie made no reply although the grammar jarred again. Oh, if they would only now go to bed

79

without argument; the necessity for energy-taking discipline.

"Whichever gets off their shoes the first can stay longer?" Jo tried again.

"That's not fair," Kitty objected. "I'm made to wear boots and you'll have your shoes off quickest."

She always had to wear laced-up boots against bad weather, chilblains and rough roads. Neither of them had made the slightest stir yet to take off boot or shoe.

"Mam," started off Jo again, "the one that . . ."

"Oh for God's sake," Nelly jabbed vehemently, "Missus, they're deleerus with sleep—they should be in bed long ago."

"Ah mind your own business. You shut up." Kitty snapped at her.

"How dare you!" The razor reprimand from Minnie was ostensibly for the rudeness to Nelly but really more for Kitty's previous intransigence. "Both of you, not another tittle out of you; conduct yourselves. No impertinence. To bed the two of you."

Kitty went to kiss her mother; this she did every night, row or no row. Minnie stooped to meet her with an unrelaxed face. Never humble with the children. Jo went upstairs, Kitty to the room near the kitchen where her parents slept; her own room above the kitchen was given over to Eily for the time being.

In her parents' room she twisted restlessly in the narrow bed against the dividing wall. The only light was from a Sacred Heart lamp, a very small one that made queer shadows everywhere. Sheamus's old pipes on a fretwork rack turned into demonic projections. The picture of John the Baptist and Jesus playing in a wood was no comfort at all to her: they were saintly, sinless children, having no common ground with someone like herself.

In the kitchen, men had gradually gathered; a few of them had sacking across their shoulders tied by strings from the top corners over their chests. Not at ease with Minnie, they were more inclined than usual to shelter under their headgear although two did take off battered hats and hung them on their knees. Sheamus, back from the yard, stood taller than any of them; his fine head, with heavy white hair, poised in unconscious dignity and eminence. The collar and tie he wore, the second-best suit, made another difference between him and the men.

They were to take his cattle to the fair tomorrow when they took their own; a few relevant matters had to be talked about. Minnie was sitting under the hanging lamp, rapidly mending a trousers of Jo's; she wanted to get to bed fast out of the men's way. Her fine-featured face was set, severe, in tiredness and tension. As soon as she was ready she put the trousers over the back of a chair.

"Goodnight to ye men, I'll leave ye to ye're own affairs now."

Nelly and Eily had already gone upstairs. Minnie went into her bedroom and began to undress. There was a mumble of masculine voices from the kitchen and an odd clear word after she had closed the door. Kitty pretended to be asleep. She could hear her father's voice and some of what he was saying, giving instructions to the men. The pricing of cattle, the way men traded in them, meant nothing to Kitty except the small break in the daily household habits these transactions sometimes made, such as tonight. She heard Sheamus in a sudden access of affirmation, very loud and definite: "Juss so, juss so."

Repeating himself, working to a crescendo, his way of emphasis when talking off-guard among those with whom he was at ease. But Minnie was always on guard for him. Even now, she put her head through the bedroom door to sizzle in a snapping whisper: "Stop shouting, Sheamus."

But he was too taken up to hear her. His crescendo had now developed a slight stutter, sign of strong feeling.

"Always k--keep a c--civil t--ton----"

"Sheamus, Sheamus," Minnie hissed a blistering whisper.

He turned towards the bedroom door, vaguely realising he was offending in some way but puzzled as to the nature of his offence.

"Haaaaa?" he shouted flatly, "did you say something Minnie?"

She was instantly furious, her so-frequent state relating to him, but because of the men she didn't break to open abuse; she contained herself to sissing like an angry gander, making full use of all sibilance.

"Stop shouting, Sheamus! For God's sake, stop shouting. The children are asleep. Can't you conduct yourself?"

In the kitchen there was immediate silence. Minnie jerked her head back through the door; she knelt down by the big iron bed to say her prayers.

Kitty lay there wondering about her mother, why she was always so easily angry, why so snappy with her father, giving him no ground. A broad big man, twice the size of his wife. She was hungry with an ache for her mother to show more love; she wished her words would not lash so fiercely at sensitive places; if she would only give her a cuddle sometimes, lift her up, even stroke her hair. Anything that would convey she understood her troubled, fighting, frightened daughter . . .

Minnie, at last between the sheets, made a long broken sigh and kept her still tense hand bunched over the rosary under her pillow.

. . . why, instead, did she always seem impatient at signs of Kitty needing her? The child ached emptily.

In her mind's eye she could see that in the kitchen her father would droop his great shapely head and blankness would settle on his face. Her mother often had this effect on him.

And in truth, Sheamus had lost the thread of his gusty instructions to the men. But they—one or two of them his own cousins from down the fields, less fortunate as to opportunity and education —realised the position and with the sometimes bland diplomacy of men such as they, handled the situation adroitly.

"Tis all right, masther, we knows what oo was tellin' us. Keep a civil tongue in our heads, that's what oo was sayin'. That's what we'll do, surely. Lave it to us—'tis good adwice. Goodnight now masther."

They chorused variously according to the degree of their familiarity with him.

"Goodnight sir."

"Goodnight masther."

"Goodnight Sheamus."

The springing spirit had sunk in him; he was relieved to be finished. He left them and came into the room and began getting ready for bed.

The men continued to sit around the warm kitchen; there they would remain until breakfast. They might or might not fall asleep. Kitty was still very much awake although lying quiet now. Her imagination was enlarging the picture of the men sitting around the fire, waiting for a black morning start. The desirability of that kind of vigil surged her already heaving thoughts. She longed with all might and main to be out there by the fire until the alarm-clock jangled awake Nelly who would then come down to cook a hefty breakfast of pork-steak and black pudding from yesterday's pig-killing at Pat Mick's over across the rae.

She dozed and woke to hear the clang of iron frying-pans on the range.

Nelly was up and putting to cook the thick home-cut porksteaks, the well-filled black puddings with their strong stuffing of pinhead, blood and onions.

A few of the men had fallen asleep in odd postures and Nelly prodded them awake with the poker.

"Now bhyes, fine maarnin' t'ye."

She thrust the big kettle towards one of them: "Now Mickeen, go down to the buckets and fill up the kittle from the spring-wather one. Make sure 'tis the spring oo're fillin' wit, an' don't be pizenin' us wit' rain-wather."

"Yerra in shure, fill it oorself," said Mickeen; "isn't that what oo're here for? Aren't oo here this maarnin' to make us our brekush. Well go on an' make it. We have our day's hardship before us."

Nelly knew she was out of luck and went herself to fill the kettle.

"A dyin' man wouldn't ha' much hope of anyone here gettin' him the preesht," she yelled at him over the splashing.

But Mickeen was pleased with himself. "Dyin' man? Sthrappin' woman. Fine pair of collops."

He prodded her calves with a long stick specially cut for the fair, and Nelly liked it. The proximity of all the men was stimulating. She flirted, strident:

"Damn oo. Was oo' sayin' hardship? Not much hardship for the likes of oo. Blagaardin an' boozin' more like."

In the bedroom Kitty could smell the black pudding cooking. It must be a great feeling to be having breakfast while it was pitchdark night outside. But she'd never know. She would never be let do it. If she did venture out there no one would want her. Even the two cousins from down the fields wouldn't want her and it was out of the question for her to take the delight of this breakfast, cooked over the roaring range while it was nightdark outside the kitchen window. She knew very well Nelly wanted the men all to herself with Minnie safely out of the way, for once.

A horrible loneliness of being so young weighed in on Kitty. A loneliness of being separate from the marvellous world of the grownups with their often incomprehensible talk; their half-sentences eluding her, yet full of meaning for them; their secret shades of understanding and interplay of jokes over her head; their brutal desirable laughter.

Minnie and Sheamus were asleep. She was in miserable isolation.

Unaccommodated Man

Geoffrey Barnes settled with his cider. It was around the time when Kate Treacy might be expected. He called her "Deborah's friend"—Deborah was his wife—or "a civilised woman", on occasion, when her name cropped up. If she came to the pub at all on Fridays he and she usually got talking. Sometimes she came late: one of her AFP—Association of Friends of the Poor—ideas had held her up, she would say. She had a reputation for tenacity in fund-drives, for some success in getting the most out of connections, managing to bring in donations even from the U.S.

The pub was fairly old. No change had ever been made in the original name, Rourke's, and successive owners in the past decade played up the age of the place in their blurb to the Tourist Board. The latest decor in neo-regency gave emphasis at strategic points, in gilt and careful navy blue, to the date of birth.

Geoffrey was in a newly furbished angle, his

bookish shoulders recessed, his soft pot pro-tuberant. He shunted the table a little to make a navigable distance between his solid short thighs and the wrought-iron awkwardness under the marble top. A large American in a pale macintosh at another table close by, seemed to find himself cramped. He stood up, holding his tankard, and nodded at Geoffrey who appeared glassily absorbed in a study of the date over the bar. Geoffrey was known to dislike what Americans did with the English language—Kate Treacy, he was heard to grant, was different having somewhere in her genes an instinct for correct usage which extended to not being crudely rich, and introducing to one only civilised people. Besides which, she had lived so long in Kilkenny.

A few touring Americans were normally to be found somewhere in the bar. They heard of the place before ever they clinched the round trip. It is possible they liked to be able to say they had chatted up the regulars, but they kept their ex-changes judiciously timed, the local business of standing rounds not seeming to be in their plan.

"You look to have more room. Mind if I sit there?" The large man indicated the padded mock-tweed bench curving beyond Geoffrey's knees. "Why not?" Geoffrey said with no encouragement but the American seemed to take the words as the endorsement required to speed him into his new seat: this old chap looked likely, perhaps. Geoffrey's head and clothes sat on him somewhat arrestingly. The toupée, for example, muddyish brown and unhappy over white fine-haired temples; the purple waistcoat; the insufficient trousers. These things were signs. One might associate them with a peculiar sort of arrogance and, yet again, they were not without unsureness. They offered promise of the interesting contradictions of the eccentric. Then too, Geoffrey had just paid for his drink: he drank slowly, so another round was due distance off.

Whatever the man's intentions were, he did not offend with any of the intrusions, breezy, lugubrious, or otherwise, that someone in Geoffrey's case might have reason to fear. He proffered no banalities of conversational assault but sat consideringly, even gravely. When Kate Treacy came towards the table it was the American who first hailed her, saying: "Hi Kate, old friend," and Geoffrey said: "The man who has mastered irony is a king over situations. I shall never be a king, Kate."

She was a thin dark woman with the high flat cheekbones that makes one think of a Red Indian. She sat slowly down by Geoffrey's other side. "Well ..." she said to him, making small tight noises, the sort of laugh that stirs pity or irritates according to how it is heard. She turned to the big man: "That embassy took care of everything then, Dale?"

"Yeh," the American said.

"This," she said to Geoffrey "is Dale Stamer ... married into my cousin's family. He's here on a business visit. But," she looked as if Geoffrey surprised her, "you already seem to know one another."

"As from now ..." Stamer left a gap of possibilities. Without smiling he somehow brightened. He might have found the woman's presence an improvement on his first position with the odd chap.

"We do not," Geoffrey was precise, "*know* one another, but since you, Kate, tell me ..." The toupée made a round little snap towards Stamer who duly reacted with: "I look on that bow as adequate inclusion, only—I do not have your name yet."

"It is Geoffrey Barnes." Kate told him. "The name goes back to Wexford and the bloodiness of Strongbow. I'm giving you history."

Geoffrey was gazing into the mirror behind the counter at a point where Kate's chin was active against a bottle of scotch on a shelf. "The name," she was saying, "goes back with the de Lacys, the Prendergasts . . ."

"The name," Geoffrey took her up, "is likely to be found, or was, until the days of the supermarket, over any little back-street huckster's shop. There were of course those in the tribe who did the right thing by the Reformation, hence a field or two which we still seem to own."

Stamer wagged his head up and down, a man assimilating. Things were perhaps turning out sufficiently anecdotal.

"You will not need to be told about his books, of course," Kate said, "coming from what you do."

"Indeed I *have* heard, but have not—I must apologise—have *not* read . . . When I go back home I'll have to be a lot in libraries, then . . ."

"Some of the books can be got in paperback here now," suggested Kate.

"Sure, but when I go back home I have to be in libraries . . ."

"A bloodless output, mine, of an unnourishing order, useful doubtless only in that it supplies evidence, should anyone require it, of a practically defunct species, the Ascendancy academic. Heh-heh-heh." Geoffrey presented his line of defence.

"I was sure," Stamer said, "the Jews were not

the best at it." Since Geoffrey gave the impression of momentarily reconnoitring Kate, asked the begged "What?"

"At making jokes against themselves," Stamer said, with the air of one delivering a bon mot.

"Ah, our little weapons," Geoffrey drank some cider to the little war with life. "Of course I could equally state myself in terms of someone else's disadvantage. We make capital of one another all the time although my aunt used to say we must not. At this, he gave his particular laugh into his cider.

"We are in perpetual business, dialectical materialist or not—makes no difference, the results add to the same. We are in the eating business. Devouring, maw-cramming. Bland mouths or frank predators, all at it: each in turn, preys."

"Let us pray," said Stamer, not seeming to mean to be heavy-footed. Geoffrey, arcing a hand somewhat pontifical, went on as if there had been no interruption:

"Let it be recognised that there is no altruism. Everything we do is an attempt at our own amplification. No matter what face we give."

"It appears to me," Kate Treacy said, an element of pleading about her, "that we constantly search for a release from the compulsion of self."

"What release can there be but the acknowledgement of our condition? The acceptance, the placing of predatoriness, of parisitism. The only brake is the recognition of our edibility." Geoffrey's gaze sank into the rise of his belly. "Then," he continued, "mistletoe *is* beautiful; the leaves, so pure an outline, the berries, so curiously at once opaque and lucent. There is a certain mystery attaching to it. One can understand why it figured in pagan ritual."

"But I refuse to be reduced to the limits of mistletoe," Kate objected.

"It is not a reduction."

"There *is* a longing beyond appetite," her thin neck showed cords of insistence.

"And what is that if not still appetite? Another aspect of the same? One must distinguish the beauty of appetite: it is the perpetuative urge."

"Yes: but I mean hunger for real perpetuation beyond mere survival? Mere on-the-spot survival? Annihilation, if necessary, which could be really dissolution into a larger whole."

"You mean into a nothing h-o-l-e. We do not need to be afraid. Anyway one looks at it, it is the urge to survival—of meaning. Nothing is also meaning. Why plead? Poor Tom in rags, diminished, was more accommodated than Lear. I do not altogether agree with Donne. Every man's death also increases me. My death increases some area." He stopped. Kate's hands were loose around her coffee-cup. Stamer looked down amongst the wrought-iron involvements beneath the table. "Our diet, of course," Geoffrey continued as if looking over a sheet of statistics, "is badly managed. What we do not get, with all this devouring is a sufficiency of nourishment. Who knew about full nourishment? The ascetics did not, the hermits, the scourgers; Machiavelli did not, nor Hobbes; Schopenhauer, nor Nietzsche. Does Sartre? Perhaps Christ was the nearest shot but then, of him, the churches have made a travesty."

Stamer's carefully conserved drink was almost gone. "You certainly make me want to check on that," he remarked. He proceeded to get up and straighten into his height while he said, "Which reminds me, I have a lot of another sort of checking to do—you know, Kate, all that stuff in South-West Cork." He gave her a handshake, then he turned to Geoffrey: "I'm sure glad you never brought up Watergate." He delayed a second, then said, "Bye", and moved away to the door.

"The efficacy of a light macintosh and roomy pockets," Geoffrey muttered.

"Said, no doubt, with nourishing charity," Kate commented.

"Said with due affirmation and celebration—of universal energy, in one of its presentations, which in this instance happens to walk about in a light macintosh with roomy pockets. Just another presentation, another form, like you, like me, or rather, unlike—that's what's so good: the permutations, the variety—Jim Griffin is yet another form . . ." Geoffrey's gesture included a man, with a mottled close beard and bald dome, who had slipped into Stamer's place. "Jim Griffin, who keeps a studio in my house, my friend, friend to Deborah."

Jim Griffin's Aran sweater carried splotches of dried clay. He kept a hand spread over each knee-cap and looked first around the pub, then fully at Geoffrey and Kate, in turn, before nodding to each, "Geoff, Kate", with deliberation. His way of stocktaking was that of a person with a sure sense of self. "Don't talk to me either of Watergate—I heard the man: who was he by the way? But no matter. Don't talk to me furthermore of converted cottages in West Cork. I have had a morning of exclamatory clichés." He dismissed the banal morning with a not-too-intolerant hand. "The only good thing today was the girl I saw leaving the exhibition. She had red hair and a woven cape to the ground. With a smile and a swirl she was gone. As a result I was cast briefly into a pleasant melancholy. I am still savouring it."

Geoffrey appeared for the time being to have relinquished the ground to Griffin who, ruminating, continued: "I really believe I actually prefer women with bond, some bit of bond. You, Kate, are too spare. To truly please me, you must fatten up. You must eat, Kate."

"Atrocious, atrocious," Geoffrey murmured but it was unclear whether he meant Kate's thinness or what Griffin said. His glance stayed a moment —perhaps involuntarily, on Kate's lean chest and, after, went along the side view of her haunches, whether in pity or dispassion would not have been easy to say. He spoke to Griffin:

"Jim, Kate looks *interesting*, like someone whose passions have been burnt to control in fasting fires. She is heh-heh a slender challenge. She would make an excellent model for a medieval piece. Why don't you use her as a subject for one of these church commissions you get, edify some parish priest in the West with a modern version of the anchorite abbess? Kate would look impressive in chaste drapes."

Coolly, Jim Griffin examined her, point after point, like someone making an inventory. "Maybe," he said. Then he made a short grunting laugh. "The control, I suspect, is not as severe as you choose to suggest," he told Geoffrey. Kate scrutinised the inside of her coffee-cup.

"I really started out saying she looks challenging," Geoffrey emphasised. "That is valid. It is impossible to take pleasure in the company of a woman who does not challenge some area in one. Deborah used to be so stimulating, although . . ." he stopped a moment and, giving the effect of some reduction, finished with, ". . . it is now no comfort to me, her

93

knowledge of Japanese."

Deborah and he had spent years in the Far East. His work on dialects was said to be commendable. People used to hear him say that what first drew him to Deborah—who was, indeed, very passionate —was her facility as a linguist. Implicit in the comment was the suggestion that he had believed they would have such common ground when the high tides receded.

"Deborah and I," Kate reminded him, "are doing our usual Elder Citizens' Programme tonight. Every Friday we do it. Remember? We have had a good week's research." There was a quality of protection against disclosure in her tone: it could have been that she was nervous of confusion in the stony places between Geoffrey and his wife.

"I left Deborah tinkering with cassettes and stuff," Jim Griffin said.

"Yes, you have access." Geoffrey observed. "An accommodating woman, Deborah."

"I am disturbed," Kate said, her hand leaving her cup and squeezing into a narrow boniness. "I had hoped—though only last week, mind you— that I had arrived at a point of inner quiet where I was beyond minding what people said, and see, after all, I have not. People like you, Jim Griffin . . ."

"Objection," Griffin broke in, "there is no inner quiet in the woman who talks that way: 'someone like you Jim Griffin'. Barbs. Contempt in that, cancelling out the serenity I imagine you mean."

She went on, disregarding him: ". . . someone like you, Jim Griffin, and you, Geoff." She used her chin, listing them, "people who . . ."

"Heh-heh-heh," Geoffrey supplied, and the sound seemed to have the effect of making her suddenly think better of her attempt at description.

"I am being very silly and exposed. I do not need to give my reactions regarding you," she said, arranging a smile.

"Right," said Griffin, "the dangers of fog; the introspective labyrinth."

"I liked the Japanese, so much," Geoffrey declared, "So ordered. Their wisdom was organic. They would never leave a hinge broken. Any disrepair was seen to at once. Prettiness prevailed. No ugliness."

"How odd then this," Griffin was pulling a magazine out of his pocket. He whipped back a few pages. "Take a look at this." The feature was on Japan: its clever photographs showed squalor, deprivation, sardonic faces of the unemployed who lay strewn about a pavement looking cynically at the camera.

Geoffrey ignored the material. "When I was there I became impressed with their concept of suicide."

"It answers nothing at all," Kate said. "We must preserve the positive. That way is negation."

"But you, of course, don't understand," Geoffrey protested. "It is moral conviction. You ought to see it their way. What is more positive than the éclat of a man who makes a clean sweep of his bowels?" Geoffrey's hand was a sudden knife around the circle of his sizeable belly. With a thump he showered his guts on to the table. The pint mugs leaped a little as his fist came down. His eyes widened to their limit and had a look that some might see as faintly crazy.

"I'd like some more black coffee," Kate gently called to the barman. But he seemed not to hear. Not many were left in the pub now. Soon the holy hour would start. The barhands were impatient for their departure.

"I must go to the Museum." Geoffrey, seemingly empty, cleansed and calm after the clean sweep of excision, was the first of the three to move. "A further area of browsing. It's what I mostly do these days."

When they were out in the street they walked in the direction of Stephen's Green. Geoffrey stopped at the corner. "I suppose I'll be around here next week, Kate. In the meantime I'll doubtless happen on you somewhere with Deborah in your ministering procedures."

"Very possibly."

The men nodded sideways at one another; Jim Griffin moved on a few steps then stopped for Kate to catch up. "I'm due at a function up this way in about twenty minutes," she said. "There will be drinks, speeches—the usual. A bit of showing-off all round. But I may be able to get a few people steamed up about a plan I have."

The air was soft. As they went through the Green the sun warmed late roses. Kate stopped by a seat in front of some and said, "I'm going to sit here a while—so mild. I expect you need to move off; there must be odds and ends you should see to about your exhibition."

But he sat down. "I'm staying a bit, a few minutes just—because the place, the air, the hour agrees with me." Lunchtime strollers had gone and it was too soon for explosive afternoon school-children. A few mothers, looking pleased in the mellow ambience, aired their toddlers.

"I feel a need to be quiet before the brittle occasion ahead," Kate said; her air was one of perplexity. "I am thoroughly weary of the way I shallow up, socially. I watch myself showing false at these things . . ." She waved indefinitely in the direction of buildings off the Green. "The hollow non-being of social fronts, the ridiculous ploys to impress. I so often swear I'll be different and, even so, I see me again and again betraying my own better sense; my own centre of quiet."

Griffin had nothing to say to this immediately. After a while he said, very seriously, "Hm. Yes. So long as this centre of quiet includes tolerance. And is not ascetic. Nor precious prim. The trappings, the tatters, the battered flesh—I am them all, I use them all in my life, in my work. The total thing."

"Tell me more," Kate said. She did not seem at all facetious.

Griffin deliberated over the patch of path between his knees. "When I sculpt I attach the wheeler dealer's face to his stripped vulnerable carcass; I balance Mrs. Murrough-Walshe's expensive rejuvenation with her reamed belly, her dropped bottom. Not in caricature; just in statement. My sort of statement. This morning at the gallery they were talking about my 'comic vision'. One can't escape clichés like that because they are so true. I wouldn't be a sculptor—that is, at any rate, turn out the sort of work I do, if I didn't accept the mixed bag, all the crazy tangles, women—although Deborah has been a longish-term woman for me —so many things. Take Geoff; subtract his books, his name, hairbit, and there is a man rejected. Months and months since he was in her bed. She forbids him altogether now. Sometimes he asks to come into my bed—vicarious aura of Deborah. I do not refuse." He shifted about like a man ready to move off. "It might sound like I have been homiletic in reverse? That'll never do. 'Bye Kate." He gave her shoulder a large light shake. "There's to living," he said, and went along the path by the Yeats memorial.

Enthusiasm

"What can they be living on? What does *he* do?"

"You saw the deerhound," Martin Gaffney said. His latest whiskey was almost finished. He shifted his chair nearer the long window that gave on to a path and a sweep of the glen going east. Trees, on one side, went to a height beyond view. A table and bottles were now closer to his hand. The time could have been between half-past two and three in the summer morning; the pine trees were navy-blue. "It sleeps beside the wagon at night."

"That doesn't answer the question."

"It does. The deerhound is what it says, for killing deer. That is, *he* kills—he has a rifle—I thought you saw it this afternoon, or maybe he had it under the mattress by the time you took a look—the hound gets them into position, and then he shoots. Mostly at daybreak, I believe. They live on that."

"But are there that many deer? And isn't it illegal?" Tom Casey, spread on Sybil Gaffney's cushions, a youngish man in softening condition, was asking the questions. Sybil laughed now, a short little screech.

"They are not bothered by the legality." She had been using vodka for some time. "Anyway Phyllis always liked secrets. Childish. Guns under the ticking—the sort of thing she'd like. Phyllis and I—by the way, Casey, did you know our mother gave us those names for the honour of the business? They were popular in the circles when our father made his first big deals."

"Deer do damage," Gaffney was answering Casey: it was as if his wife had not spoken. "The ethics are quite good really. Someone must destroy deer. A question of priorities. They increase enormously. Proportion is the thing. Foxes too. There is a great deal of nonsense purveyed about blood sports. If I were a fox I'd rather have hounds chase me than be victim to poison. I could at least be able to run to earth: I'd get that sporting chance."

The girl beside Casey said, "I can see how Phyllis might want to try this other sort of life, with him." She was sitting without leaning on the yielding surfaces about her. Her foot, which had been turned up beside her on the couch, she now removed from under Casey's hand by putting it back into its clog on the floor. "Something more . . . elemental . . . requiring struggle."

"Biddy, we came from struggle," Sybil said: she had put on a version of a Lancashire accent. "That is to say our grandmother struggled, and our father always told us that he struggled harder again, pushing fiercely to make his pile—to the result you know, business and property all over the place, even to unshakeable interest in this country of his adoption. But he certainly had to struggle."

"Only you did not," Gaffney said, allowing her at least a parasitic existence.

"Everyone struggles," Casey declared. "Let me be trite and say it: struggling takes different forms. Isn't that so, Biddy?" The girl, who at no time had shown response to the ready bottles on all sides, was watching the brightening sky: she did not answer him. "I don't have to remind you, Martin," he went on, "that your wife must have had her struggles." He turned comfortingly over the back of the couch to Sybil, standing behind, and stroked her arm.

"Private ones, Tom." She leaned towards his consolation. "Like Phyllis, whom therefore I should not, I suppose, condemn, I have my secrets."

Gaffney looked from the window to regard the pair of them; he gave an appearance of indifference.

Biddy was wearing a long dark garment, the sleeves of which reached to her wrists. She stood up now and moved into the increasing light coming from over the glen.

"You remind me of Phyllis," Sybil said, watching the young girl; she sounded a little less shrill. "She always wore dark covering-up things, neck, arms, legs, everything, everything covered. Unnatural in anyone not a nun . . ."

"Nuns don't cover anymore," Casey broke in on her. "Their collopy calves are for all to view, and frequently no addition either. Very Mullingar. Best left to the imagination as previously."

No one made an amused noise. Biddy went back again to the couch but she now sat a few inches further from Casey.

". . . that was why my mother was so badly hit when she went off. People—my mother, father, everyone—used to think she would be the solid parish-worker type. Next, there is nothing. Total blank. Disappearance. Nothing until rumours of a wagon, a man, a baby, a wandering life—you saw them out there this afternoon. I'm surprised she risked herself this close after that long gap."

"A proud difficult silence?" said Casey.

"We knew hardly anything. She never looked for money."

"We did pick up the odd thing," Gaffney supplied. "We knew he was American. And I must say I did not totally dislike what I saw of him over on the hills today."

"In reality he is probably quite cosily doing," Casey suggested, "with a Yeats thesis stashed away in some academic repository, and is giving himself a long freak-out sabbatical. The question then is, could it be a proud difficult silence?"

"For whom difficult?" Biddy asked, rejecting flippancy. Gaffney filled out more whiskey.

"I am only asking," Casey told her. "And you Biddy, are anyway too young to know."

"No younger than she must have been when she left . . . but I don't know if I should be brave enough . . ."

"Brave?" Sybil threw the notion aside. "She was indulging; no different from me in my other sort of way. It takes no special dedication, what she did—none at all."

"And she got the baby and you . . . got all this." Gaffney's glass circled to suggest the room, the house, the grounds about.

"With you included," Sybil's scratchy laugh came once more. "Not to forget what I brought you. Those ground-rents via me are not unwelcome, respected and all though your profession may be."

"From my couched position," Casey considered,

"the life-style of Phyllis and her man seems desirable in certain of its aspects."

Gaffney had put down his glass and had begun to prowl. He suddenly asked, "Will we go over?" No-one answered. "Over, I said?" He jerked his head at the window, the sharp movement like a deliberate counter to previous langour.

"Where? On earth, where?" Sybil said and her tone was that of someone dealing with a bore. She thrust her flimsy shoulder between the two on the couch, attempting their collusion. A shift short of distaste occurred in Biddy's face and she resumed her looking at the sky. Casey said, "Sybil, you are fairly fluthered."

"Wine only," she said, showing the vodka.

"It is a shame to turn liar with the divine essence," Casey told her, and Gaffney took him up at once.

"You are right. Regrettably, we do not put the Bacchic force to proper use. Of old we would by now be having a sacred ceremony—I mean having thus far imbibed." He stood so that his saddened plumping shape showed against the glass. "Out there, we should have been."

"This is entirely true," Casey agreed. "We degenerate, lounging in our plush. Of old, we would have had a significance to our drinking. Sacramental."

Biddy was very serious saying "I would like to believe it could be . . . sacramental. I feel too this . . . degeneracy. Abomination." Over the carpet she was shaking a hand free of nasty slime; she did not look at the people with her.

"Rubbish." Sybil dismissed her; she gave them all a cigarette laugh. "Never. Our Saturday evenings here after the races are a . . . ritual, if you like, but ha ha ha sacramental, never. Ceremonial? . . .

103

allow me as you are my guest . . ." With elaborate movements she fetched for Casey a bottle off one of the tables and proceeded to add to his drink. "I'll ceremonially fill your cup . . . but . . . nothing is sacred . . . anymore. Ha ha, except of course the fantasies of Gaffney. Dear Martin . . ." She made a theatrical bow to her husband.

"We should be out there," Gaffney said again, refusing the invited reprisal. "We must make an effort towards regeneration. The occasion is propitious. St. John's Eve."

"How versed of you to know. I married you for your well-stocked cells."

"In fact it is not St. John's Eve," Casey was positive. "But it makes no difference. All our dates are fabrications anyway."

"All our dates are eves to something or other," Gaffney offered the obvious without pretention. "We shall go now to find Phyllis who could be said to have chosen the better part." He grasped a bottle by the neck and walked on to the stone ledge beyond the window. Without delay he began an uneven canter down the path. Sybil, in her minimal dress, rocked after him shouting "You bloody fool, Gaffney, you know you love your cheques."

"We must," while he turned back, saying it to her, Gaffney's empty hand moped into a young tree after some supporting bough; his pink shirt was panting over the small rise of his stomach, "we must attempt a return to the pristine. See the dawn is far advanced!" His unsuccessful hand left the tree and indicated the lyrical sky. "Now is our necessity to seek the dawn of things again. The primordial significance."

Casey, like an echo, took him up. "Significance,

yes!" He was close behind Sybil and at that moment stopped to blow on his glasses and focus afresh on the primordial dawn. Biddy, remaining a minute at the open window, her fingers still holding the frame inside, looked back at the stale room and then, unsurely, followed in the downward procession.

"The Bacchants . . . hi Sybil!—Martin will tell you this—Martin will tell you the Bacchants were based on enthusiasm, the early meaning of the word." Casey's insistence invaded the morning. "The fruit of the vine," he explained gustily to the dewy shades, "made possible the godly feeling, the deity incorporated—that's what it means, enthusiasm."

At the far side of the glen, beyond a pyramid of granite, they straggled on the open circle where the caravan was, yellow and clear red against the heavy green of the wood. Alongside a fire of sticks a huge hound lay, head on forefeet. Phyllis and the man were sitting on stumps. Neither they nor the hound made any noticeable change in their positions at the approach of the party.

"Phyllis, you elemental," Sybil gasped, "Biddy thinks you live the elemental struggle . . ." One strap of her dress hung down her arm, a released breast burgeoned where given leeway.

"Phyllis," Gaffney said, "you must tell us things . . ." The girl at the fire still sat; the man, his long hair in a plait, stood and said "You could wake the child."

"Ah the child!" Sybil breathed and stared down at an infant asleep in a wicker basket slung between branches.

"They say you kill deer," Casey said. Biddy was regarding the camp from the encircling grove. The man did not answer. "At dawn . . ." Casey continued.

"It is hardly likely, is it?" the man queried. "Have you seen deer hereabouts? And if you have, would they be likely to stay with all this racket?"

"We are depriving you?" said Gaffney. "You are really accusing us. And you are right. But there is hope . . . we are in search of new energy. We seek the pristine ecstasy." He swallowed from the bottle and let it drop to the moss at his feet.

Phyllis picked bits of bracken off her woven skirt. "Your usual Saturday search," she said. The words were more in the nature of a matter-of-fact question than a comment. She had hardly looked at her sister. Biddy had come closer and quietly studied the child. A rustling was set up in the trees in the last few moments; it could have been owing to a little local flurry of air, or to a tethered horse. Gaffney, staring into the noise, made a speculation: "A deer?" Then, "That is no deer. And we could not ever, ever catch, by our poor soggy selves, a deer. Never, with our naked hands. We must settle for . . ."

A rabbit frenzied across a short arc of the circle. "A rabbit, yes. We could manage a rabbit. Possibly." The hound had loped into the thicket.

"We should have vine-leaves in our hair and grapes about our ears," Casey shouted. Snaps of dry wood cracked as he lumbered after Gaffney in the direction the rabbit had taken.

"Jesus, Jesus Christ," Sybil made a reduced moan. She clutched a swath of drifting ivy and began to swing out of it in silence. Biddy walked once near Phyllis and the man standing close to her, and then returned to sit by the cradle, her head touching the wicker weave.

When Gaffney and Casey returned they swung

between them a terrified rabbit. "There was a strange beast. The hound . . ." Gaffney's gesture intimated possibilities on the hill. The hound had not come back. "But this that we have captured must be torn, limb from limb. Devoured alive." Without much breath he had been attempting a fast, rising chant. Casey, something less winded, followed him up, achieving a climactic urgency.

"In re-enactment; in commemoration—as the Titans tore and devoured Dionysus, the god that disappeared and was born again, we must eat of the living flesh. This is the sacred orgy, the sacramental Bacchic feast . . ."

"You are depraved. Sick. Sick." Biddy, sobbing, had snatched a brand from the fire and was striking over and over the hands that held the rabbit. The small creature fell to the ground and, after a weak spasm, lay quiet.

In the valley an early bell began.

Normal Procedure

"I hate being circumscribed," Miss Gormley said
out loud towards the cage. The balding magpie in
it answered in its way. Miss Gormley was wearing
green tights and a longish narrow skirt with a slit
up the side. She had been wearing the same skirt
the previous day when the Dean had brought up
the matter of appearance at the staff meeting. It
had been one of her more obviously braless days
also. They had been becoming more frequent
latterly at the school.

Miss Gormley told visitors she did not keep the
bird as a pet. She ached for the poor thing she
would say. The cage was the lesser of two evils,
the second of course being death.

At the meeting a certain obliquity regarding
moral standards had slipped in among the other
straight items. The Dean had emphasised that the
school, categorically, was not the sort of place
where a particular kind of whistle from a boy might
go unreprimanded. Castigation of the exciting

causes of such a whistle was left almost totally to inference. The Dean had gone on to stress the necessity for the inculcation and preservation of decorum as a counter to unsavoury trends everywhere threatening.

The bird Miss Gormley had found, a maimed fledgling. She had refuged it, tended its hurt, and by the time it was mended it carried the taint of captivity and could not be allowed loose among the predatory hazards of the urban trees. The man who lived with her that month happened to have, among other unlikely oddments, a Victorian parrot-cage. He gave it to her. She also gave him favours, lightly bestowed.

The parrot-cage and Miss Gormley's care combined did not add up to natural processes and the magpie, although cheerful, was undersized and poorly feathered.

Miss Gormley continued talking towards the bird, "So I'll damn their eyes again." As she said it she was pulling a tight sweater over her naked top half. "I'm off," she said to the man reading, still bedded, on the mattress. She leant across him to snatch an opened fan from its slanted arrangement on the wall. "I'm taking this for them to draw to-day," she said. "Have something nice —lasagne and chianti, say—ready for me. I'll be starving. To-day is my longest in the week, remember?"

"You'll get fat," he said. He was a dark heavy man.

"No fear. Anyway I can afford to. So make it lasagne."

"What'll you do—for all these comforts—when I'm gone—next week?"

"By then I'll be due a change. By then it will be

time to sample someone else's cuisine."

She delayed a second by the door looking back at him. He did not appear to give her any of his attention. "I'm just off," she repeated, "but first I'll hang the cage outside—or maybe you might do it for me?"

He said, "I saw some perfect specimens of her kind dive-bombing the cage yesterday. They hate the ragged creature that she is. For her difference. As far as those free proud ones are concerned she is a deviant. Survival demands destruction, obliteration, of a functionless deviance. Or what appears to be that."

"You may be quite right." She said it airily. "In the meantime the poor thing needs at least the air, if that is about all of her natural condition she can have. Hang her out will you?" She got no further comeback and she said, but amiably, "Oh you . . . I'll put it out myself." She swung the heavy cage on to a wall hook outside the window. Quickly then she caught up a striped straw bag wherein were some of the things of her trade. On top of them she dropped the fan and hurried out of the room.

But she did not get out of the house immediately. Mrs. Bailey was in the hall. "I am actually going, Miss Gormley," she said. A small travelling case was at her feet. She went on in little flurries, "Amazing, isn't it, that I have actually managed it? I have said goodbye to her. I give her the best of my life. What I mean is the best I possibly can. In the ten years of her life I have never taken a day off with peace, as I've often told you." The young blind girl she was talking about went past Miss Gormley, her elbows angled outwards, while with hands sensing the space before her she made her way upstairs. "And now I'm actually going . . . for over a week."

Miss Gormley said nothing for a while. She looked up the stairs to where the girl's older brother stood on the landing. As his sister came close to the spot where he was he turned his head away, and when her stretching hand came near him he moved back to the wall. Miss Gormley said then, "I should have thought time off was essential. Surely there are places to take care of her while you get away?"

"There are—is—there's the Institute. But I always have these worries, these anxieties about her. I know, I know . . . you'll call me what everyone else does . . ." Mrs. Bailey fluttered an unhappy hand towards the ceiling, ". . . neurotic. All right. But I'm going away now for a week and . . . I have fixed things up. I've said goodbye. Goodbye again, Tom . . ." This to the boy above them. ". . . and the taxi is to be here in a minute—in fact it *is* here." The wham of a car door was to be heard outside. "Goodbye again, Tom." The boy still gave no word but watched her go, his narrow face out of the light. Miss Gormley also called goodbye in her fashion and then rushed along.

The Dean was not a fat man. When he was anywhere juxtaposed to people of either sex whose swelling flesh was conspicuous his celibate features took on an extra reserve. One might infer from his face at those times that such manifestation of the human shape was an offence, even an obscenity. Energy in any burgeoning form appeared to upset him. His function was one of control and under his jurisdiction energy was required to operate within the framework of his prescription. The special leather implement in his righthand pocket gave witness to his dislike of certain schoolboy departures from that framework.

Miss Gormley saluted him, "Hello Dean." It sounded brightly but seemed to be a manner of address to which he did not freely respond. He made his brand of harnessed sound at her as she sped on to the staff-room. There the break was in usual swing. At one end the men talked football and hangovers. At the other, the women were entangled in the matter of black tights.

"I hate them," one teacher said. "School stockings finished me with the black."

"You went to a convent school?" Miss Gormley asked; her air amid them could be said to carry the protection of insouciance.

"Didn't we all?" the first teacher said.

"I love the black ones," Miss Gormley said, untroubled. She had been heard more than once referring to the "experimental" school where she herself had been. "Especially the see-through sort. They look super with red."

"Yes, the red-light area." The teacher, saying it, pressed close her calves in their safe beige.

Miss Gormley gave a general smile and said in the lightest way, "It's a pity the religious life has imbued black with such schizoid connotations." She plonked down her bag of Italian straw and took out the fan which she flicked open, her bright green leg flashing a step or two.

"My God, but you're the giddy girl this day with your St. Patrick's Day green."

"I love colours—experimenting—on the leg." Miss Gormley insisted.

"And you have the leg for all that too," one of the men called, distracted from his football.

The class-bell rang and soon the staff-room was empty but for two of the women whose exchanges continued into their free period.

"Our friend Miss G. upsets the Dean."

"She may have another thing coming too."

"Of course one allows that art teachers tend to be that bit different, but . . ."

"Indeed. You can say that again. I have had the pupils bringing up some of her ideas—in my opinion to no-body's advantage. In fact a number of those in her class were definitely disturbed trying to figure out what she meant by saying the devil is a projection of private and aggregate fantasy."

"What business has she bringing that sort of rubbish into the art class? I'm certainly glad none of my children have her for anything. Supposing, just by some freak, supposing she got civics to teach, or *religion* . . . God! doesn't bear thinking."

"There *is* the problem that she lives so close. All the pupils live around; there is nothing to stop any of them knowing . . . She could have the decency to keep herself private."

"But it's clear she doesn't give a damn what anyone thinks. Actually she even makes a point of . . . well, you could say . . . brazenness."

"You have seen the set-up she lives in?"

"Mmm. Who hasn't? She invites the world. No reserve. What most struck me was her way of having everything different from the way any normal person would want it—old water-pipes deliberately laid bare—that sort of thing: she says she likes their *configuration*. And she doesn't go for TV, and she has never understood the need for a fridge in this climate, and she has taken down the partition so that the bathroom is actually part of her main room."

"That's because, as she puts it, she likes to observe, have everything open to her, while she relaxes in her bath."

"She roared laughing the other day when I was telling about our getting the new teak front-door —she sets great value on all that old moth-eaten stuff that looks as if she hauled it in from God knows where. And then the mattress actually down on the floor! The size of it, too! The day I was there she had three boy-friends in tow."

"You know I can't but feel more and more that things should be put to the Dean. Plainly, I mean. We have the right of objection to staff-conduct. A standard is required. This sort of irregularity, looseness, is a matter of . . . of . . ."

". . . of scandal?"

"Exactly. Not to be countenanced. To be rooted out."

Miss Gormley walked down the school drive. At the bend of the hill the gate stood open. A tree beside it was splendid; alone and strongly spread. Against the sky its stripped branches, patterning a light stone colour in the March sun, could call to mind something of a cathedral; not any of the gloom, but the aspiration, the triumph of delicately achieved masonry. At the high point of the arched tracery two magpies sat making every few seconds their kind of rattle, a repeating short harshness proclaiming a winter vigorously won and a fresh urgency. The two of them gleamed clear health, white and black. From a little way over the roofs, from the hanging cage, an impoverished eager magpie sound came to meet their regenerative insistence. The pair of handsome creatures rose and flew in sharp spurts to a point above the house where Mrs. Bailey and Miss Gormley lived, and then they both swooped decisively. Miss Gormley began running down the hill.

When she reached the door she several times missed the keyhole. As she was finally managing to twist the key a large object fell past her from somewhere up the wall of the house. It made a wild terrible cry which made Miss Gormley turn and look downwards. Below her on the basement strip of concrete Mrs. Bailey's blind daughter lay twisted peculiarly. A whiff of cooking garlic came on the air.

While the ambulance was on its way the child croaked once from under Miss Gormley's shawl spread across her on the cement, "Tom . . . did . . . it . . . Tom . . . pushed me out the window." A good deal later when the girl's broken legs could be left to nurses Miss Gormley took up her first hurry to the cage. She found the rickety bars strained away at one side. The pecked bloody bundle inside was not yet altogether cold.

The man said, his hands trying to make a beginning and end ". . . I had gone to get the wine . . ."

The Requiem

Cold cold grey, the vistas of the city lay below the window.

Her back was to where he stood in the middle of the room.

"Bleak eesn't it?" there was mockery in his question. She knew he would say something like that before he spoke. At first he had repeatedly surprised her with intuition of what was in her mind—bleak was what she was now thinking, feeling—and then she was surprised no more. She remembered others of his race who possessed a similar quickness. It is a racial thing, she thought, his sudden readings of me are without sympathy. So she made no answer. If she were to turn and look into his face at that moment, it would only be to know another uncountable time, pain: the eyes looked soft, and promised, only because they were made that way—some game of nature—they yet fulfilled no searching out from her; what she had mistaken for warmth was only the dark pig-

116

mentation of genes, convening from dark foregone generations.

She did not answer but continued to look over the January houses and trees.

"The bleak mees-under-standing world," he mocked again. "Yet it ees an experience, ees it not, the cold, the bleak-ness?"

Even the way he said it, his characteristic way of breaking words up oddly, syllabically, set pain moving. She loved the way he talked. She still answered nothing, but stayed as she was, standing in her stockings on the end of the bed where she had gone to fix the hang of a curtain. She remained turned away towards the window.

Why should she bother coming to him? Why, when there was so much else she had to do, so many people to see, did she come? Because always there was a challenge or always there was hope? She wasn't sure. At first there had been much hope, before she had known to despair the barriers of his self-protection. What had happened to him? Where had it started long ago? What made him so afraid to be vulnerable? Perhaps an inane question that last. Who wanted to be hurt? Not she either, but she felt at least she laid herself more open to life—that maybe it was better to do this since otherwise there were only armours and masks and no touching the reality of people?

He came behind her, putting his arms about her. Against commonsense hope stirred, a small movement, frightened before it began. He drew her down on the bed and in the very instant when she longed to feel a wanting in him speaking through arms, feet, clothing, he took one arm from around her to click on the record player handy to the bed.

"Brahms' Requiem," he said widening his hand

now lightly around the top of her head.

Is being with me like death for him? Yet she did not speak. Were she to ask that fear-generated question out loud he would use it to hurt more. It would be quite in his usual style for him to say facetiously Ye-es you have keelt me, or, I am already dead—dees you know, I am a—wreck.

But he would not tell her simply why, at this time, a requiem was what he wanted them to hear. Perhaps it was not one simple reason.

To the still high room the sounds of the city scarcely reached. So low he had turned the music the magnificent chorus arose into the room's dimness as a remote unearthly harmony, ravishing her. Such beauty was anguish.

O God O God, she cried inside herself, so much I do not understand.

Lying together, his arms again around her, they were separate. He suddenly joined in the German voices, leaning on one elbow. It was a loud unexpected noise, a little deprecatory. She was not in his mood but, as often when with him, because of her bafflement at his refusal of depth, she gave something from the shallows.

"You told me you didn't know German." Pathetically coy.

"I don't."

"But you sing it as if you knew it."

"So? The words are weeth the records. I play them only five hundret time." Droll.

She waited, thinking about his many hours retreated in his lofty tidy room, taking in music, absorbing it like air, not knowing even that he was doing it. He had said the first day he brought her to his room,

"I do not like to bring people to my place."

118

"Why?"

"I think it should be better place."

"It is fine. I like it. So quiet."

What she was really liking was being able to see what his room might tell of him. It told something. A little. It was unstrewn: a few garments disciplined over the back of a chair; cupboards closed; newspapers folded; no clutter. In a broken rectangular pattern he had covered with the help of brass drawingpins, one entire wall in sheets of gift-wrapping. This wall both startled and woke pity in her. His tiny kitchen was bare, whitely bleak: a new tablet of soap—a good brand—sat on its flattened-out packaging on a corner of the naked enamelled table near the sink; a razor, a toothbrush, each cleanly laid on the porcelain sink edge; a couple of straight towels. A small kettle on the stove; a cup with a light residue of black coffee, and one clean spoon were at the other end of the table from the soap. His essential solitariness was spoken in the icy kitchen that was also washroom. There was not even the suggested comfort of evident food.

"The Cath-o-lic Church forbids sex and forbids death."

He was serious as rarely and in silent eagerness she listened. She was hungry for anything that came from below the protective mockery, the baffling sallies, the wearying almost puerile wisecracks. "I think there is here connection. They equate sex with death, mortal sin, that archaic stuff. They forbid life—sex—and therefore they must forbid death. That ees why they preach eternity."

"It is a new notion to me." But why was he playing the Requiem? "It bears looking into."

Something had almost killed the ultimate in sex for him. She was watching his face where suffering had done some work and she found this face beautiful. She thought: I think you are lovely. But she dared not say it. Yet she heard herself saying while her finger followed the line of his mouth, "I think you are lovely," and it was as she had feared when she had sensed it would be foolish to speak. He lay back on the covers and took her words. Narcissus seeing his glorified image in her eyes. She put, with no calculation, her fingers on his trousered knee and lightly as almost not doing it, but with every longing, drew them slowly upwards on his thigh, inch by asking inch. When it had been with other loves such a yearning movement had crescendoed to impassioned eyes, rushing limbs, searching mouths. But Narcissus turned his eyes to the ceiling, only once, fractionally, giving her their belying hurting softness. She put her hands together and sat in a droop on the edge of the bed.

The small gas fire did not heat the room.

"It *ees* cold," he said and took off his shoes. "I must be warm," and he was talking waggishly again. "The bed ees a warm place. I must be warm."

He put his trousers on the armchair before the fire.

"Come come, be warm," he was drawing her beneath the covers and she yielded because of a crouching hiding hope. He cannot help it she was thinking, excusing herself. Pride is of no use here. It will find me nothing. I need to find. I can't accept that there is no way.

So she lay in his tightened but still uncomforting arms. His embrace was sometimes impersonal, mechanical—a reflexive process developed through many women who were also kept outside the walls of his feeling self? Or had he ever defencelessly, allowed some to see and know him? Questions.

Hours went and their clothes were scattered on the floor about the bed. He seemed to be almost asleep.

"I am tir-ed, I am tir-ed," he repeated over and over. "My mind is tir-ed. Exhaust-ion through frustrat-ion." She was also spent. Ineffectual struggling.

And then a sound quite other from his ordinary voice which was strong, male; he crooned almost as a nursery song, scarcely to be heard, "Rien à faire. Rien à faire." Four or five times he repeated it, eyes closed, hands holding each other on his chest. And she too, after a few minutes, echoed once very quietly from him, wondering was that what he helplessly felt. Was she for once being allowed to hear beyond the extra defence that English had become for him? He mostly avoided, even rejected his natural language. But she was mistaken. His eyes were watchful, aware, when they opened and he, deliberately mishearing and mocking, took her up:

"Of curse it ees unfair."

He was taking her nowhere with him. With held-in anger but more pain she said,

"You could never live with somebody day by day and take the burden of knowing her; face the test of letting her know you. How could you sustain a woman? Little relationships that go beyond no titillating fringe, that is what you want? You are sealed in an iron box and I can find no chink in it. You don't want me to, of course, do you? But people have to stay more or less open to be any sort of people—fuller that is. Else it is a closed life.

One might as well be dead."

He did not answer and his eyes were closed again. Since their time together she had said too many nice things. It had been hard, in spite of clearer judgement, to keep from saying them. His returning comments for her, however, had no extravagance. Once he slashed at her saying,

"You see everything as too col-oured. You do not look at things as they are. You do not see what ees real."

If she said now some of the hard things that were also true, might that possibly crack the encasing enamel? Encounter the agile evasion? She began to try.

"So I don't see what is real? I see that you are just a vegetable. This room answers your contracted needs once you have collected your vegetable wages. You need scarcely stir outside it. Your fire which barely does, your books—and even those you say you do not want to read anymore—your music which you say you tire of also, your bed, your meagre amount of food to keep you alive. For what? Why do you want to stay alive? What amoebic abortive existence is it? You do not want to meet anybody—really meet, I mean. What makes you go from day to day? You might as well not be there. You could die up here and for a long time no-one would know. They might come to collect your rent maybe, and when they had taken away the negative remains that was you, someone else would take over your room. It would be as if you had never been."

She was wanting to hurt only to be able further to tell him he need not be this way at all. She could then know the pleasure of having him gratefully listen. To her telling him there were some answers for him, did he but want them. "Could you straighten *me* out?" he had once asked; but he was laughing at her, at someone they both knew who had asked her opinion, her advice on a problem. Maybe he had felt a grain of jealousy but if so, never in a thousand years would he admit it.

He was lying on his face when she had finished talking. Completely still. But it was not the stillness of sleep. She wondered had she, hoped she had, wounded him. And almost at once was sorry also. She leaned over him, bending her head down to his but she could not see his face. Calling him, her voice was a whisper. His swarthy shoulders barriered her but after a while he said out of the pillow,

"You must forgive me . . . but I am cry-ing like a leetle bébé."

Yet his body was still. His weeping was a private inward thing. She was for that more sorry still, but also glad, because of the confession that even such exclusive weeping was. He was confessing himself vulnerable and that was the first real hope. That their bodies had known no zenith together had not been tragedy, but his refusal of innerness had been her near defeat. With a tentative cheek to his shoulder she said,

"I thank you for letting me see that you can cry. I see that as a privilege. I only said those things to try to reach you some way, even in hurt. That I have hurt you, that you *feel* what I say, oddly helps. You have staved me off for so long, side-stepping, evading . . . there is no point in our being together if this is the way you play it. I am entirely weary of that game. Let me *know* you a little. Couldn't you be simple with me? It's really all. Other things will follow. Fall into place."

But he still refused her. There was no melting to her. His crying had been a private despair, jealously private. He was not going to allow her the indulgence of sharing. Revealing. His eyes were bright, tearless, mouth bitter, when finally he hoisted up to say,

"You have succeeded in des-troying whatever leetle confidence I might have had. You destroy it."

And still *that* was revelation although he had not meant it so. She hurried,

"O no no no, this is not what I wished to do. Surely not. I have said so much in praise of you which you seemed to take all for granted: how could you react so? To the nice things you answered I see everything too highly coloured. That I don't look at what is. What do you want me to say? I tell you the other side—and it seems to me both are true—and that destroys your confidence! I *know* you could be so different. I am certain sure you could be so marvellous, so fully rounded a person if only you—came out. It is not your body I want, at least not first. You, we, are starting at the wrong end. That is no good. Ten a penny. I could have men that way any time. You don't have to be afraid of me, I don't want anything. Yes I do—I would be really happy, in fact humble, to know you. Won't you *let* me know you?"

The record was long finished and replayed several times. Now he leaned out of the bed to set it going again and then drew away from her, haunched on his pillows. He made it plain he was not going to meet her. Sarcasm twisted out the syllabic words:

"Foolish. You see I know the way I am. You do not help at all talking dees way. There ees a blind man, a lame man—you do not say to them you are blind, you are lame. They know. You do not help to say so. I see the way I am. You do not help to say so. I—grudge you for what you do with talking. *I* see things in you but I do not say."

"Please do say. I would so much prefer you did."

"No no. I will not say."

"Why not?" A scalding shame was pouring around inside her. How stupidly precious she had been in trying to humble him; how superior. She was minus, herself, far from total. And he was cleverer than she; not accusing, only touching off her torment of self-doubt.

"I look at people," he was naked on the pillow: the room was no warmer, earlier he had wanted to be warm. "I teenk I can see what ees wrong with them but I do not say. Why? What good? You are driving a car in your town; you are the cause of knocking someone down. You do not know but you knock him down. You keel him but you drive on—you do not know you have done dees. It ees all over, there ees nothing can be done. Yet I know you have keeled this man and only I know. But do I tell you? No. What good to tell you that you have done dees harm? There ees no way out of it and it ees not your fault. It just happened. So you see I do not tell."

"But if it helps me to be more careful? To avoid future similar mistakes?"

"Leesten," impatient, "it ees not your fault. You are the cause, the un-wit-ing cause. The harm done ees not your fault. What good then to say? It ees—vanity."

Vanity? Had she presumed too much, settling herself as being more released, more developed, above him? What of her inexplicable need that drew her, when many well-springs were accessible, back and back to him who could give her so little?

What inner compulsiveness made this imbalance?

She lay ashamed, flaccid, on her stomach. The quietness of the room made it removed from the day; from life. A high-up tomb in which the unbearable beauty of the music bore in and in on her and she suddenly found herself heaving in shattering sobs. Her complex self, her husband, her children; this man and the women he knew beyond her, women he had maybe been able to love as he could not her; the knowing half-words in pubs; the suspected, the part-heard sniping at parties; the tangling intricacy with people near to her whom she loved and who resented her behaviour—weltering, banked feelings attached to these and nebulous other troubles, rose and burst from her as the muted requiem lifted and sank in breaking agony. Bereavement. Isolation. No expectancy of any tenderness from him. So far he had never been her solace so that when she felt his nakedness gentling now down upon her, holding her, consoling her, she was indeed afraid before committing herself beyond uncertain edges of happiness.

"Ssh ssh poor bébé, poor poor bébé."

He raised her onto himself spreading her hair about his chest; he lifted her face up over his mouth and kissed her long.

"Ssh ssh poor bébé I do not want to leave you empty. I want you to be happy."

He was rocking her as one might rock a troubled child. It was his kind of coming to her. For them both some synthesis out of the ragged hours.

Tomorrow she would be gone from the country. They merged into sleep.

Spectrum

Micky Gillespie lived to the east of Sallynoggin in one of those old houses still to be found there. Within reasonable strolling distance was Dunningmere where Miss Montieth and Miss Pierce-Hume nurtured. One occasionally might hear Hoorawh! from the playing fields.

At night, Micky frequently suffered hot flushes. He woke in panicked sweats that went clammily cold when he lashed back the bedclothes. Leonora, when sympathetic, said: The horrors again? Yes. Inundated with yellow and black. The sunflower is a rushing yellow and its black heart is a swallowing menace. So is Priscilla. And Dunningmere . . .

She's in your nightmares all the time. And they seem to be obsessed with yellow. Maybe we should take it down off the wall; arrange it somewhere else. You shouldn't have eaten those seeds. Too many.

No Leonora, don't move it. We agreed to eat the seeds; they are so good for us. We are what we eat.

That's why it hangs there, isn't it? A symbol.

We never said, Micky. I thought it was a souvenir of a crazy laugh one day and a freak discovery. I meant the other seeds.

On the wall over the bed it hung upside down, the five-foot stalk at a balanced slant in carefully placed hooks, its fine oval petals reduced from their first towering yellow to a neutral paleness; the heavy head with its weighted blackish heart of seed having pulled the stalk while still malleable to sudden curve. Dust grew on it day by day. Occasionally Micky blew a few rapid gusts of breath at it but did nothing else to remove the dust.

It is immensely beautiful Leonora.

Yes. Absolutely. We brought it back because it was, and because of Priscilla. She admires Magritte so.

Time to time a seed fell into Micky's hair. He might find it on the comb and, scrutinising it for accretions of dust and dandruff or either, put it in his mouth and chew it notwithstanding. Again, he might find an odd seed on the pillow or in the bed. Finding, he always ate. Leonora and he also had extra packets of the seed for eating that they bought in Patrick Street.

He and Leonora—she was particular no-one should abbreviate her name—had been driving up from Groslejac that day they lifted the sunflower from some French farmer. They had reached the more level stretches where yellow acres of the flower bulged their dark pregnant centres to the afternoon sun.

Let's stop Micky. Let's walk among them a little. The main road was miles off. They stopped and got out. There was no house in view. A myriad insects clekked and zinged. Leonora moved a little way in between the rows, touching the greyish leaves. Micky called after her, They turn their faces according to the sun. Suddenly she began laughing, a wild discharge, and pointed along the dry ochre clay to where an old sun-split tree trunk marked the outer line of the crop. Just beside the trunk, standing in its incongruity as if to the place created, was a perfectly sound white porcelain lavatory pan.

Oh Micky! pure Dali, pure Magritte! You can see where they get it—the eviscerated organ of some quotidian situation—the sheer irrelevance set amid . . . and yet it has to have relevance . . . He said nothing to deflate. Not a syllable. He even let her go on another minute.

What does it mean Micky when they do that?

Does it have to mean anything?

But it does. Everything always means something —even Priscilla. The juxtaposition of the dead trunk, the loo, the sunflower, the . . . the total unexpectedness . . .

Then he said, It's probably for the defecation of donkeys. Having said it, he used his penknife to cut the stem level with the earth, Leonora supporting the stalk. Easily five foot Micky; we must be careful with it. They put it extremely carefully into the boot, taking much pains to protect the soft halo.

We'll put it over the bed Leonora when we get it home.

Yes.

Sometimes they agreed surprisingly

Yes Micky, but let me do it. I know exactly how it should go.

I was afraid you might be wanting to give it to Sidey Bulman, Friend of the Earth.

No no, not this; we'll bring him another souvenir

from the earth of France.

Sydey W. Bulman, an American Jew and their neighbour, had for his own best reasons turned to Dun Laoghaire in his youngish retirement and had soon become an addition to the district in his Aran Tam o' Shanter. He was founder member of the quickly enthusiastic local Friends of the Earth, and rented, between Joyce's Tower and the Mirabeau Restaurant, suitable premises.

In October Micky planted scores of bulbs.

You have chosen everything yellow Micky. On purpose?

Scarcely so. I hadn't noticed.

We should have variety.

We shall. We do. Priscilla is various—when she comes. What marvellous clothes she brings with her these days.

What a good thing she comes. Twice in one year—after all that time.

She wears very fine clothes. Amazing really.

She always had taste. From the first. Precocious possibly, that subtle discrimination, but at Dunningmere they appreciated, at least, that—they are snobs that way, Miss Montieth and Miss Pierce-Hume.

Her things now, though, Leonora—this is more than just taste. This is plus. Silk. Yellow silk. Fur. She has a great flair for yellow now. That never was her choice. Yellow kid boots. She never said how much she earns.

One doesn't ask Micky, does one? Even one's child. In that obvious way, I mean. She never asked *us*.

One does wonder—those long holidays; even the Carribean. Costs the earth.

And the flat when she did allow us to see it that

last time in London. It's got everything. An air. Turkish rugs. Those originals.

She has become so polite now too.

Indeed. She kisses one also.

True. Leonora paused. She never has a great deal to say, has she?

No. Never stays very long in the room; not a great deal to say. True. Gets restless. Very quickly. Moves about if you ask her questions.

One wonders a great deal. One can't ask two questions running . . .

. . . she is gone if one does . . .

. . . doesn't seem to like conversation much.

But she does visit. She *has* returned.

*

The sun shone down the Burma Road and the walls of Dalkey Quarry glinted at points. He might take a walk in the woods; maybe up to the obelisk. Passing Dunningmere—the origins of the name were uncertain—Micky disliked afresh the new nameboard. I am not a snob but I dislike it. I am not a snob but it gives me satisfaction to feel superior to their announcement of themselves. Before, they did not need to put themselves so obviously in the general eye. They were even smug in their sureness of clientele. Some of the boarders lived in castellated stone houses, old properties of the Pale. It was put abroad that their claim went back before the Statute of Kilkenny. Priscilla knew all about that stuff. If at no time impressed by it. Always used to cut things down to size, Priscilla. All that silk and kid and fur latterly . . . Yes, that stuff about the Pale, the Fitznormans of Castle Norman, the Bartletts of Bartlett Manor—that sort of thing went to make the ethos of Dunningmere . . .

Leonora, Miss Montieth has such square grey hair.

Such a heavy tweed bottom Micky. But now that she has become a Friend of the Earth, that's entirely in keeping.

Miss Pierce-Hume is curly to her straight.

Bony to her padding, Micky.

She is the swivel to Miss Montieth's ordinations.

The endorsement of pronouncements.

Why have we Priscilla there, Leonora?

There are some benefits Micky.

*

Mummy, they call Miss Montieth "he".

Who? The seniors?

I am a senior now Mother, don't forget.

True. Well then, you know some parents take that kind of he/she thing as typical slagging.

Some parents—the two and three car group. We have only an old jalopy.

Sharp you are Priscilla. Micky, do you hear her?

Yes. Needle-sharp. On the point, Yes, some parents take that kind of precocious teacher-slagging as part of the Dunningmere quality—part of what you pay for. There are not that many schools to choose from if they want something of an air; they take Dunningmere such as it is, crumbling wainscot and all.

*

Crumbling wainscot within but the approaches, at least, were impeccably kept. Not a single dandelion.

Dipped lawns and judiciously placed weeping ash, mimosa, eucalyptus. One was made somehow to imagine colonial sunshine and servants bringing China tea under the shade. It was pleasant that in summertime, through an open front window, Mr. Guest, the music-teacher and something of a name, might be heard composing on Miss Montieth's best piano.

Come on Priscilla, put in just twenty minutes. You know you owe it to the privilege of having him as tutor—another ten minutes . . . just ten.

Mother! Rubbish! Privilege nothing. Have you seen that greasy little twist he wears his hair in up the back of his head?

Sh-h . . . genius is often eccentric.

Genius rot! Does *he* have a niff! Whew! You've not had to sit under him on a hot day.

Genius *can* smell. It's allowable.

*

Then, too, Dunningmere did insist that one should cheer Hoorawh! at games, and, at all times, elocute elegantly. That had advantages. Wherever, after, one had reason to cheer one was likely to reflex in the refined fashion. At Trinity, for example, beautiful vowels were useful even if one took up with the hard left—all the more proof of how enlightened was one's relinquishment.

Father, Mother, it is not so much that I dislike Dunningmere as that I endure it. So boring. There *have* to be distractions.

Micky, Miss Montieth wants to see me. In her

133

mahogany and leather study.

I'll come too, Leonora. I'll arrange things to be free then. It's our only child after all.

No Micky. She didn't ask for you. I'll handle it.

Ah Mrs. Gillespie . . . please come in. Miss Pierce-Hume is here also. I have already spoken to Lady Bartlett. It was with one of the Bartlett twins—Louisa—that Priscilla . . . If Mr. Guest hadn't overheard . . . He was invaluable with his car—no need to call in the police—found them up at the lead-mines' chimney. Fortunate that we had such staff cooperation; isn't it so Miss Pierce-Hume?

Entirely.

So in view of what happened Mrs. Gillespie . . . and you know, this is the *only* time—Miss Pierce-Hume will bear me out? Yes—the *only* time I have asked to actually see you specifically about . . . in view therefore of what occurred I should like to ask you . . .

You do not need to at all Miss Montieth; we had planned on Priscilla finishing this month—a really good thing has become possible for her—abroad.

What did you say the good thing was Leonora?

I didn't Micky. No need for the indulgence of detail. Miss Montieth & Co will tell it their way in any case.

We must make some arrangement quickly . . . get something planned for her—London—Paris . . .

No Micky. No possibility. There is no arrangement you *can* make. She has gone already. Tonight.

And no goodbye?

No goodbye. One needs to know when to let go.

*

. . . passing Dunningmere he disliked afresh the new name-board.

There, surely, is Miss Pierce-Hume under the larches, exercising Miss Montieth's Alsatian. Zipped to the chin in this holiday weather. Cleft to the navel like the victims of Cuchulainn's sword— depends how you see it. Not the type of female I greatly take to. Nor the other one either. And those excruciating Christmas stage efforts—ye gods! A bunch of . . . but one must not generalise. Never generalise . . . good afternoon, Miss Pierce-Hume. Splendid animal.

Yes, yes. Invaluable against the Nogginers, you know.

You've had trouble?

Not since the second dog; we've had to get a Doberman Pincer—for the back entrance. One would be so vulnerable otherwise.

I can imagine. Violence everywhere.

Miss Montieth exercises the other one. Violence everywhere indeed.

Indeed yes. A woman in the train to Killiney yesterday had her eye gashed with a bottle smashed through the window.

Horrifying, Mr. Gillespie.

Yes, totally gratuitous. Splendid animal.

He is. We have to keep him and the Doberman separated. Loathe one another. The territorial thing, you know.

Quite. I understand.

I sometimes *see* Mrs. Gillespie. Priscilla is . . . ?

I must move on now. Nice to have seen you again; not for some time, has it been?

I suppose not. Priscilla . . . ?

Oh . . . splendid. Thank you. Well I must move on.

135

Going over the slope are you? Well you may find Miss Montieth on the far side.

Dutiful, that's the appearance Miss Pierce-Hume presents. A creature long-practised in turning to genteel account what lies within her perimeter. Her rear has however—curious I hadn't noticed it before—a peculiar undulation, a rebel nuance of vestigial seduction... Ah Miss Montieth! My day for encounters.

Good-day Mr. Gillespie.

What a fearsome specimen! They eat one, don't they?

I shan't let him do that, have no fear; I believe in being civilised—wherever possible, that is. We keep hearing about your experiments, Mr. Gillespie.

You do?

I was really on my way back for some tea; would you like some?

Why not? Thank you. How do you spend your summer holidays Miss Montieth—apart from the Cyclades?

Well, Hart Crane really, this year; and then, my spinach, leeks, and rockery.

Crane?

Well, I've been commissioned to ghost-write on him.

For—

Oh it wouldn't be ethical—he must be nameless if famous.

Quite. Understood.

So, since you ask, I do a few hours on Hart Crane, then an hour on the leeks—the hoeing is good exercise—another hour on Crane and then the spinach, and so on. I love it. Highly suitable combination.

Sounds as though it should be.

In a work like that one has to be aware of the pitfall of caricature.

It is an attraction to be avoided.

Tea in a moment Mr. Gillespie. And Priscilla . . . ?

Ah thank you . . . I think if you don't mind I'll change my mind about taking tea. I'd better be getting back. Leonora will be . . .

Mrs. Gillespie is well? I sometimes *see* her at the Friends of the Earth.

Yes, she's well. Thank you.

Priscilla?

Splendid. Doing absolutely splendidly. I must be off. Goodbye then. Good to have seen you again.

. . . and, Leonora, I said Good to have seen you again, and do you know, I meant it. One can misjudge so badly Leonora.

True Micky. Oh by the way, a package came for you from Priscilla—special courier again—we'll be having pickets outside the house at this rate—her delivery this time was Dandymack Daly from Cabinteely; flew in for a few hours.

Is he her newest?

I should say he is more likely to be history. Open up the packet; its bound to be for your birthday.

It *is*. Excellent taste. A beautiful edition. Marvellously illustrated version. I'll keep it for tonight. Just now I must deal with *them*. Just see the absolute hordes of the things that have sprung open since morning!

All day the sun had shone and a thousand new dandelion heads burgeoned to meet him after Dunningmere, overpowering lesser life. Three times since the first decapitation that year they had arisen. Everywhere the juicy leaves flourished as if never even threatened, let alone poisoned, decimated, burnt. The seeds were indestructible, infinite. Already, the crown of one shorn, scores of secret seeds were sprouting against him. Under the lilac tree they stood in ranks, laughing at him with their strong yellow faces. I shall do it again, he said. There will be a great sacrifice. The knife.

Don't dramatise it Micky. Come with me instead.

Where?

To the Friends of the Earth. A sound orientation. Good way to pass a holiday hour or so. You could continue your positive thinking—after Dunningmere. Indeed I sometimes *see* Miss Montieth there. Come on.

No. Not away from here again today. I don't wish to dissipate my precious hours unnecessarily —all that waffle.

You never want to come with me to these things, Micky.

Should I?

Don't you feel the need to be stimulated?

You can't be serious. Where in Dublin is there anything that is socially stimulating? Such superficial yabbering! As you well know, I'd far sooner be in my own—to me—entirely agreeable home with all the things I most like around me—books, music, trees. One gets so exhausted with all that banal small-change.

Micky that's being separative. And anyhow, as I've told you before, it's never like that at Sidey's club. *Some*times, I say *some* times, what you pejoratively call banal is essential; it's just people's way of reassurance; in its apparently trivial way it represents something of the eternal value of salutation.

Bull. Leave me, woman, to the garden. Space.
The bliss of thought. I mean to deal with the triffids.

A knife he had said. Leonora saw him with it as
she went off. Addressing the first dandelion he
gauged Micky said, She has so many things to
occupy her. A launching here; an opening there;
little talks to Voluntary Bodies; a preview; a poetry
recital. With all the stuff in my briefcase, I cannot
keep up with her. I don't want to keep up with
her. She's off, cheap, to Nepal soon. Thinking of
her incessant busyness is somehow weakening. He
lifted the strong green coronna in his left hand
and thrusting the knife down parallel to the root,
gave a slanting slicing twist. The etiolated small
stump left in the ground bled a little, whitely.
Micky told it, I feel a little stronger now that the
gate has shut behind her sludge-toned skirt and
petunia scarf. She supports culture with an almost
aggressive negation of personal adornment—except
for those scarves. Strange trailing things. He continued plunging and slicing, rarely getting to the
long embedded root-tips. Or alternatively—depends
on how you see her—she pursues culture with an
admirable lack of personal embellishment. Her
well-risen stomach is in full curve, unrestricted. No
elasticated foundation for her; no shoved-up
rolls about her waist nor congested thighs. Her
undisguised natural swell is commendable.

Milk gathered and wept from broken stems.
Truncated friendships, Micky said to the rising pile
under the withered lilacs, that is what they remind
me of. One by one he cut and cast. Some kind of
rejoicing was going on down around the People's
Park; amplified conflicts of John Travolta and
O'Donnell Abu clashed and, minimised on the

southward-floating sea air, came over the green, white and yellow carnage in the Gillespie's garden. Articulators from the provinces, devastating towards the ferry, took total dominance; the summer ambience trembled at their passing and succumbed to noxious exhalations.

Among the remaining dandelions the tortoise inched its infinitesimal way. It was immemorial, the previous owner of the house, a literary bachelor, had said; it would be an offence against evolution to remove it; there was, he said, a smell of perpetuating power where it chewed its minimal way through dandelion bloom. So, a bonus to the sale, it had been bequeathed along with the proliferous powerful flowers, and Micky had many times, with hour-long fascination, studied the endless enigma of its old old head and brilliant flicked eye. From Leonora's careful corner a sunflower plant was swelling to promising bud. There should always be, at least one, Leonora held, for so many reasons. I'm tired, Micky said to the sunflower.

*

Miss Pierce-Hume! I hadn't expected . . . so you've joined the ranks!

Oh I've been a member, Mrs. Gillespie, for some time; ever since Miss Montieth joined, really, even if I haven't always quite made it to the meetings.

Sidey does say the membership expands.

Mr. Bulman, is, I think, quite a crusader. Well anyhow, today I have come *and* I've brought a rather special contribution—recommended to all! It's udder cream. They use it all the time on the Bartlett's farm—for the paps of nursing cows . . .

Fascinating!

140

Nursing cows here, Miss Pierce-Hume?

Ah Mr. Bulman—excellent for the hands, that's the punch. Mrs. Gillespie you remember the Bartlett twins?

I am not likely to forget.

E-euh . . . naturally . . . Well, the estate is gone now, you know; only a few fields left; everything mortgaged—the father died in the DT's. Supposed to be very hush-hush but we all knew.

I must tell Micky. Very sad.

But Louisa—you will remember her then, since she and Priscilla used to be rather friends?—well Louisa still occasionally comes to see me and yesterday she brought me the udder cream.

Too sad, indeed, about the father. But the cream . . . you mustn't think it unfeeling of me, but ha ha ha it's too killing!

Excellent for the hands. I saw Mr. Gillespie today. Tired-looking I thought. All that new experimental work, no doubt. A trifle strained-looking. He overworks, I imagine.

It's his temperament to do so. And he doesn't sleep very well. Starts awake suddenly and can't sleep again. Perhaps you, Sidey, could recommend something from your nature lore? Some natural remedy?

I shouldn't want to pronounce Leonora. No panacea. Perhaps he lacks iron. Why doesn't he try eating dandelion? That is, he oughta tell 'em why he's eatin' 'em and that way he'll get the best outa them.

Really Sidey? How marvellous! Right under our noses all the time.

*

A voice said It was a dream of white blood. Micky looked to see the voice and it was the sunflower. Eat, it said, eat them.

Leonora shook him awake beside the thousand dandelions that bled under the lilac tree in a dark green pyramid blobbed with wounded yellow. The tortoise with great dignity and the beautiful deliberation of all time ate through one of the still standing heads.

Oh Micky, you have left so few; scarcely enough for the tortoise. You ought not to annihilate, Micky; they are your allies. Eat them, Sidey says; it's a good idea, he says, to chat them up, ask their help before you eat them. They'll help you sleep—it's how you do it that counts. Look at their amazing faces—full of sun: that is the function of their yellowness; they are another kind of sunflower, don't you see, and they are maligned, they who are the friends of man. You must read up Apollo again, Micky, this time in Priscilla's present to you. And Micky, the clocks, those diaphanous clocks . . . you used to tickle me . . .

Leonora I have always recognised the perfection of the clocks; don't drown me in castigation Leonora. Too bad I fell asleep. I should have saved it for tonight. Let's have some tea.

Sidey suggests you should cut down on your tea intake; begin on dandelion. Tonight we are going to have a dish of dandelion to go with supper—sieved, and with a little butter or a dash of cream, it is delicious. Better than spinach. You will sleep. After all, people have always been incorporating in one way or another—survival, celebration—nothing new to it. Catholics make a big thing of it eucharistically. We *can* ingest to purify or commemorate.

Well, try anything once; there may be something

in what your Sydeh W. Bulman says.

There is bound to be, said Leonora taking three large flowers, and now these I mean to honour, in mollification. They will be mounted and given status over our bed along with the sunflower.

In the small hours Leonora could be heard complaining from her pillow, Why do you burst awake again like that Micky? I don't like it, being crashed out of my sleep. Is it fair, night after night?

Ah Leonora, if you could have seen how predatorily they ranged themselves in their burning yellow—and I was miniscule to their giant size. Uncompromising. No mercy. They were coming, an engulfing army of them. A nightmare full of yellow blood. Their blood and Priscilla's . . . I shouldn't have eaten them . . . perhaps I didn't explain enough, or maybe I wasn't humble . . . how could I expect anything but their hostility?

You become so vocal at night Micky; is it fair, waking me up? I like a packed day and then a full night's forgetfulness—no empty hours, the only way to prevent brooding.

Listen Leonora, *she* was in the middle of all that welter and her voice was saying things like, Father how could you judge? No-one has the right to judge . . . squalor for years . . . too proud . . . and who was there to support me and the kid? . . . I could earn easily that way . . . depends how you see it . . . in Japan it's taken for granted . . .

Micky, if you must wake me then don't carry on a delirium. Here, read for a while; forget the fantasies and read—the new book, the one she sent you today.

Yes . . . yes . . . I'll do that. It *was* nice of her, wasn't it, to make such a valuable gift to the night

Anglo-Wic FK 1520

stock? Horribly costly—the sort of thing you hold
just for joy in the bookshop, knowing you shouldn't
buy.

Not Priscilla. Not these days. She never did tell
us her earnings though, nor exactly *how* . . .

Leonora I really would prefer . . . just now,
please . . . those nightmares . . .

Yes, Micky, yes. Read, or just turn the pages.
Try to be relaxed. I'll look too.

First rate, these reproductions. But, in fact,
the pictures for all their excellent quality are
nightmarish too . . . there's Chronos—chopped off
his old man's genitals—ate his kids since they were
a threat. And here, here's a good one of Zeus—much
given to devouring their young, these mythical
blokes. Even their wives—for what good it did
them. The young always seemed to spring out
again in some shape or form: ". . . from the head of
Zeus sprang Athena, fully clothed and armed." . . .

Good Heavens, look, Micky! Look at yourself
—you look exactly like Zeus!

Opposite their bed in the wide mirror where
hung a sunflower flanked by three mounted dandelions, Leonora and Micky stared at the man with
nightmare hair and startled barrel mouth and who,
Leonora said, looked like Zeus.